MANDIE
AND THE
FIERY RESCUE

IN MEMORY OF

J MICHAEL JUSTICE

DONATED BY

GILBERT F NORWOOD

Mandie Mysteries

Mandie's Cookbook

MANDIE
AND THE
FIERY RESCUE

Lois Gladys Leppard

BETHANY HOUSE PUBLISHERS
MINNEAPOLIS, MINNESOTA 55438

Mandie and the Fiery Rescue
Lois Gladys Leppard

All scripture quotations are taken from the
King James Version of the Bible.

Library of Congress Catalog Card Number 92–73060

ISBN 1–55661–289–3

Copyright © 1993
Lois Gladys Leppard
All Rights Reserved

Published by Bethany House Publishers
A Ministry of Bethany Fellowship, Inc.
6820 Auto Club Road, Minneapolis, Minnesota 55438

Printed in the United States of America

Snyder County Library
Selinsgrove, PA 17870

Especially for
that dear little girl,
Margaret Mason Tate,
with love from "Gramma Lois."

About the Author

LOIS GLADYS LEPPARD has been a Federal Civil Service employee in various countries around the world. She makes her home in Greenville, South Carolina.

The stories of her own mother's childhood are the basis for many of the incidents incorporated in this series.

Contents

"Blessed is he that considereth the poor: the Lord will deliver him in time of trouble."

Psalm 41:1

Chapter 1 / Leprechauns?

As the boat neared the coast of Ireland, Mandie and her friends stood on deck and squinted through the mist for a first look at the country. The wind was blowing so hard they had to hold on to the railing to keep their balance. The icy chill stung their anxious faces.

"Whew!" Mandie exclaimed above the roar of the wind. She held on to her bonnet with one hand. "It feels like ice-cold wintertime and it's supposed to be summer!"

Jonathan Guyer spoke loudly, "For some reason it's always cold on the water here, and the wind is always blowing. And because it's cloudy it makes it even colder."

"I sure hope it doesn't rain," Celia remarked. Her auburn curls whipped around her face as she secured her bonnet with one hand.

"I can see Ireland now!" Mandie cried out, pointing shoreward as she jumped up and down. "And it's all green just like Grandmother said it would be."

"Even the leprechauns are green," Jonathan added with a mischievous grin.

"Leprechauns?" Mandie questioned. "There are no such things as leprechauns—are there?" She looked at him, uncertain whether or not to believe what he said.

"Sure. Just ask the people in Ireland. They'll tell you all about them," Jonathan replied.

"Do you mean to say the people in Ireland really believe in such things?" Celia asked as the wind whistled around them.

"Of course they do," Jonathan assured her with a solemn face. "And whatever you do, don't ever let an Irishman know you doubt the existence of these little people; that is, if you want to stay on speaking terms with him."

The two girls stared at Jonathan to see if he was serious. He didn't smile, returning their gaze evenly.

Mandie turned back to the railing. As the harbor came into view, her only interest was in landing and exploring the country.

Mrs. Taft, Mandie's grandmother, had brought Mandie and her friend, Celia Hamilton, to Europe during their school vacation. Senator Morton, a family friend, accompanied them. They met up with Jonathan Guyer on the voyage. So far, they had visited England, France, Italy, Switzerland, Germany, Belgium, and Holland. It was 1901, and travel was slow, but the thirteen-year-old girls were enjoying every minute of it.

The boat touched the moorings and bounced, throwing the young people back a few paces. Mandie leaned forward over the railing to look below. Workers scurried about the dock. Carriages lined up in the distance, waiting for passengers to disembark. Suddenly out of the noise and bustle, Mandie spotted a small band dressed in green uniforms. They began playing Irish ballads to welcome the visitors.

"Look!" Mandie exclaimed to her friends. "A band!"

"And they're all dressed in green. The Irish do love that color," Jonathan said with a smile.

"Green is the color of everything growing. It's what makes the earth so bright and beautiful," Mandie replied, watching the musicians.

Celia tugged on her friend's sleeve. "Mandie, your grandmother said to go back inside and get Snowball when we docked, remember?"

"Oh, yes, I'll be right back." Mandie turned to weave her way through the crowd now gathered on deck.

"We might get separated," Jonathan told her. "We'll go with you." He reached for Celia's hand to pull her along with him as he hurried after Mandie.

The three found Mrs. Taft and Senator Morton just inside the door. While the senator stood surrounded by their bags, Mrs. Taft was trying to hold on to Mandie's white cat at the end of a red leash.

"I'll take him now, Grandmother," Mandie said, quickly stooping to scoop up Snowball.

"And I'll take some of the bags, Senator Morton," Jonathan said. He grabbed two large ones, even though he was only slightly older than the girls and not very tall for his age.

"You girls can carry your small bags," Mrs. Taft directed. "Our trunks will have already been moved ashore."

The girls picked up their handbags, and Senator Morton carried the larger ones that remained. The passengers were rapidly leaving the boat, propelled down the gangplank by the rush.

Mandie, short for her age, stood on tiptoe to peer around the wharf. The crowd was too dense for Mandie to see anything. Senator Morton led them to a waiting carriage and engaged the vehicle to carry them to their hotel. The driver immediately jumped down and held the door open. Mrs. Taft and the girls stepped inside and watched as Senator Morton and Jonathan helped load their baggage.

Mandie and Celia eagerly gazed out the window while the vehicle moved ahead. Mandie became excited as they entered the business section of Belfast. Small, colorfully decorated shops lined the narrow streets. Everyone seemed to be wearing something green.

"Oh, I love it, I love it!" Mandie exclaimed as she twisted in her seat to hold on to Snowball and view the town. "I'm really in Ireland!"

Jonathan leaned across Celia who was sitting in the middle. "I'm sure you'll love the leprechauns, too, Mandie. Watch for them. Sooner or later you'll see one."

Mandie turned to him and said with a frown, "Jonathan, please stop teasing us."

"I'm not teasing," Jonathan insisted with his mischievous grin. "If you're looking for them, you'll see them."

"Just because you've lived and gone to school in Europe doesn't mean you know everything there is to know about it," Mandie said to him in a huff. She turned again to look out the window.

Mrs. Taft and Senator Morton were engaged in their own conversation and were not aware of the remarks between the young people. Mandie ignored Jonathan until he finally stopped speaking of leprechauns. Celia, always the peacemaker, tried to change the subject.

"I wonder what mystery we'll come across here in Ireland? Every place we go we seem to get involved in some adventure," Celia said with a little laugh.

Jonathan and Mandie spoke at once. "Oh, there's sure to be something mysterious about Ireland," Mandie said as she heard Jonathan saying, "You won't have to dig for something unusual in this country. Maybe we can capture a leprechaun."

Celia sighed, and Mandie glared at Jonathan as she turned her gaze outside.

Jonathan smiled. "There are so many mysteries in Ireland, we'll probably run into a different one every day."

Before Mandie could add a remark to this, their carriage slowed down and finally came to a stop in a long line of vehicles. Looking at her grandmother, she asked, "Why are we stopping? Are we there, Grandmother?"

"There?" Mrs. Taft asked, puzzled. She looked out the window and then said, "Oh, yes, I believe this is the line to our hotel. Goodness, there must have been an awful lot of people on that boat booked at the same hotel."

Senator Taft followed her gaze and said, "Yes, quite a few. Maybe you'd all like to get out and wait in the lobby while I stay with the driver until he can unload our luggage."

"It would feel good to stretch these cramped legs," Mrs. Taft said with a smile. "Thank you, Senator Morton, I think we'll do just that. Get your handbags, Amanda, Celia, Jonathan." She rose and picked up her small bag.

The three quickly joined her as the senator helped her down the steps of the carriage. Mandie held tightly to Snowball with one arm and carried her bag in the other hand.

Mrs. Taft spoke as the young people gathered around her. "Amanda, whatever you do, please hold on to that cat, do you hear?"

"Yes, Grandmother, I won't let him down," Mandie promised as they moved up the sidewalk toward the front entrance of the hotel. Then she spied a huge sign over the doorway. "Look! The name of the place is Shamrock

Inn! And there are green shamrocks at each end of the letters."

"All painted in green," Jonathan observed.

Mrs. Taft looked back to the young people. "Come on now, or you'll all get lost in this crowd."

"Yes, Grandmother," Mandie said, quickly stepping up beside her.

When they entered the lobby, Mandie gasped. "This place is covered with shamrocks!" She set down her bag and pointed to the wallpaper, which had stripes of shamrocks going up the wall.

The room was crowded and everyone seemed to have heard Mandie's exclamation. Almost every eye turned to stare at the young people. Mandie, suddenly self-conscious, quickly picked up her bag and hurried to join her grandmother at the counter. Jonathan grinned and pulled Celia along.

Just as they were next in line to be registered, Snowball managed to struggle free from Mandie's arms. He jumped to the floor with a thud and took off through the lobby, weaving his way among people's legs.

"Snowball!" Mandie cried, hurrying after him.

Mrs. Taft called after them, "Please get that cat."

Snowball zigzagged between tall potted plants, low settees, and baggage. Every time Mandie thought she could grab him he streaked off.

"Snowball, come back here, you hear?" Mandie called after him. She kept bumping into people and apologizing as she ran around the room. Jonathan and Celia joined the pursuit, but the white cat was too quick for them. He found the door to the hallway and darted out.

"Snowball, when I catch you, I'm going to punish you good," Mandie declared as she stopped in the corridor to look for him through the crowd.

Celia remarked, "There sure are a lot of people in this hotel."

"Yeah, a whole boat full," Jonathan said with his mischievous grin.

"There must not be many other hotels in this town," Mandie said, quickly resuming her search for the white cat. "Kitty, kitty!" She bent to look through the crowd and immediately bumped into a man.

"There he be!" the man said with a laugh as he pointed ahead to a counter. He had a strange accent that Mandie immediately decided must be Irish.

Looking in the direction the man indicated, Mandie saw Snowball standing on the counter licking his paws and washing his face. "Oh, thank you," she said to the man as she hurried forward.

Running up to the counter, Mandie snatched the end of Snowball's red leash. "Snowball! Grandmother is going to be awfully put out with us," she scolded.

Celia and Jonathan caught up with her.

"There's a leprechaun!" Jonathan said, pointing to a large poster on the wall behind the desk.

"Where?" Mandie said, whirling to read the advertisement. It read:

Catch a Leprechaun

See this new play at the Belfast Theater.
Limited run,
so don't ye be
wastin' yer time
tryin' to decide whither
to go or not.

"It's a play!" Mandie said excitedly.

"That it be." The man behind the desk heard her remark and told her, " 'Tis a very good play, I hear."

"Are there leprechauns in this play?" Mandie asked.

The man smiled at her and said, "American, that ye be. And sure there be leprechauns in this play. Go see for yourself."

Mandie cleared her throat, glanced at Jonathan, and asked, "What do leprechauns look like?"

The man was short, rather heavy, and had a big smile. He laughed at Mandie's question. "Ah, so ye niver see leprechauns in America," he said, pushing back his curly black hair. His blue eyes twinkled as he bent forward over the counter and explained, "Three feet tall they be. Wee little men. Their clothes be green and their hair be red."

Mandie's eyes grew wide as she listened. There must be such people if this man could describe them. Glancing at Jonathan who was hanging on every word, she whispered to the man, "What does the word 'leprechaun' mean? Why are they called leprechauns?"

"Leprechaun? It be Gaelic for shoemaker," the man explained. "Now, I'm sure ye must know what a shoemaker is, being shoes are made in America."

"Oh, yes," Mandie quickly agreed. "If they are only three feet tall, what do their clothes look like?"

The clerk bent to pull another poster from under the counter and held it up for Mandie to see. "This be a picture of a leprechaun," he announced.

Mandie, Celia, and Jonathan leaned over the counter to scrutinize the poster. The little man in the picture wore an old-fashioned frock coat with seven large silver buttons. And his trousers only came to his knees, where they met with white stockings. His shoes had large silver buckles on the tops and the toes curled upward. A three-cornered hat covered his head, and a leather cobbler's apron covered the front of his clothes.

"Isn't he interesting!" Celia exclaimed.

"Yes, and look at his face," Mandie said. The little man had piercing, dark eyes, a hooked nose, and he was grinning from ear to ear.

The clerk watched the young people stare at the poster. Mandie asked, "Are there really such people as leprechauns?"

The man smiled at her, tucked the poster back under the counter, and turned to wait on someone who stood at the other end. Mandie stamped her foot and said, "Well, he could at least answer me."

"He didn't answer your question because he wants to keep you guessing," Jonathan told her.

Mandie picked up Snowball and turned to look at Jonathan. She saw Senator Morton coming toward them.

"Miss Amanda, your grandmother is ready to go to your rooms now," the senator told her as he smiled at the three of them. "I see you've caught up with Snowball."

"Yes, sir, finally. I'm sorry. I guess we've been dilly-dallying while you and Grandmother have been waiting." She turned to walk with him back to the lobby. Jonathan and Celia followed.

Mrs. Taft was sitting on a settee. She stood up as she saw them approach. "Amanda, please hold on to that cat. We don't have time to waste for you to go chasing after him."

"I'm sorry, Grandmother," Mandie replied, squeezing Snowball tightly in her arms.

"The man has gone ahead with our bags, so let's hurry," Mrs. Taft said as she and Senator Morton led the way out of the lobby and down the corridor.

The young people followed them to rooms on the ground floor. Mandie and Celia would share a bedroom again, with a sitting room between their room and Mrs. Taft's. Jonathan and Senator Morton had rooms farther down the hallway.

As everyone separated, Mrs. Taft said, "We'll just have time to change clothes before supper, and then we'll take a walk afterwards."

They all agreed to meet in the sitting room when they were ready.

Mandie and Celia went into their bedroom and closed the door. When Mandie dropped Snowball to the floor, he immediately rushed around the room to inspect everything.

"Oh, I wonder if there's a sandbox for Snowball," Mandie said, quickly looking around. There was a door beyond the bed, and when she opened it she found a bathroom. "Oh, thank goodness, there's a box in here. Come on, Snowball."

Snowball followed her and immediately found the sandbox. Mandie went back into the bedroom and flopped onto the huge bed. All the furniture in the room was oversized and heavy-looking.

Celia was already rummaging in her trunk. "Mandie, we'd better hurry so we'll be ready by the time your grandmother is," she said as she lifted out a bright green dress.

"Oh, so you're wearing green," Mandie said as she bounced off the bed and went to her trunk. She unlocked the lid and opened it. "I wonder if I have anything green to wear," she said, flipping through the dresses inside.

Celia looked at her and asked, "Are you going to wear green, too?"

"I sure am," Mandie grinned as she stood up to shake out a white voile dress with green polka dots and trimmed with a green velvet ribbon.

"Oh, that's pretty," Celia remarked as she began slipping off her traveling suit. "We'll both be wearing green."

"Well, we are in Ireland, you know, and that seems to be the color here," Mandie said with a big smile, as she shed her crumpled traveling clothes.

The girls quickly dressed, and brushed their hair. Celia wore her long auburn curls loose with only a narrow ribbon to restrain them. Mandie quickly braided her blonde hair into one heavy plait.

As they stood before the long mirror, Mandie asked, "Celia, do you think there really is such a thing as a leprechaun?"

"I just don't know, Mandie," Celia told her. "I've heard of them, but I've never known anyone who actually saw one."

"I can't decide," Mandie said, shaking out the wrinkles in her long dress. Then she remembered the poster advertising the play. "I've just got to ask Grandmother if we can go to see that play, *Catch a Leprechaun*."

"Yes, that would be interesting, I'm sure," Celia agreed as she surveyed her reflection in the looking glass. "I think Ireland is going to be one of my favorite countries on this trip to Europe."

"I agree," Mandie said. "I love it! And I haven't even seen much of it yet." She turned to look at her friend and added, "You know, just because he has gone to school in Europe and traveled around a lot, Jonathan thinks he knows everything."

"But he's bound to know more than we do. This is our first time in Europe, Mandie," Celia reasoned.

"I don't imagine he's ever seen a leprechaun, though," Mandie said.

Snowball came bounding out of the bathroom, jumped up on the big bed, and began washing his face.

"Well, neither have we," Celia reminded her.

"Celia, can you keep a secret?" Mandie asked excitedly.

"Of course, Mandie," Celia replied.

"Please don't tell Jonathan, but I *am* going to find out whether there is such a thing as a leprechaun or not," Mandie told her.

"You are? How?" Celia questioned.

"I don't know yet, but before I leave Ireland I'm going to find out if they really exist," Mandie replied.

"I've heard tales that they are very elusive, if there are such things," Celia offered.

"I figure between the two of us we'll be able to track one down," Mandie said.

"The *two* of us?" Celia asked, a worried look in her eyes. "Suppose we get in trouble with your grandmother?"

"We'll be careful," Mandie promised her. "We won't have much time though, because Grandmother wants to go on to Scotland, remember? We'll just have to hurry."

"Here we go again," Celia moaned.

"Right now we'd better see if Grandmother and the others are ready to eat." Taking a last look in the mirror, Mandie thought about how she would stop all that teasing from Jonathan.

The girls opened their hatboxes and took out bonnets that matched their dresses. Mandie left Snowball in the bedroom, promising to bring food to him and take him on a walk later. He objected with a loud meow as his mistress closed the door.

Chapter 2 / Molly

Mandie and Celia were the first ones in the sitting room, but they had barely sat down on the settee before Jonathan appeared in the doorway. He smiled at them and flopped into a chair near the door.

"You girls really look nice," he told them with a grin. "I'm surprised you could do so much in such a short time."

Mandie frowned and looked at Celia, who was clearly puzzled.

"Are you saying we were in such a disreputable state from the journey that you didn't think we could improve our appearance in time for supper?" Mandie asked curtly.

"All of us were in sad shape when we arrived here. After all, that was a long journey from Holland," Jonathan said with his mischievous grin.

Mandie opened her mouth to protest, but Jonathan continued, "Just look at me. I still don't feel presentable."

Mandie laughed and asked, "Presentable to whom? You look all right to me."

"Thank you, but you haven't noticed," he replied, sitting up straight. "My jacket doesn't match my pants. The one I should have worn was too crumpled to put on, and I couldn't find the pants that match this jacket. So here I am, rather mismatched."

The girls laughed.

"Mismatched?" Mandie could hardly tell the difference between the navy blue jacket and the blue pants. "We've seen you in worse condition," Mandie reminded him. "Remember when you fell in the water in Belgium?"

"Well now, if we're going to dig up mishaps, how about the time you fell into the lake in Germany?" Jonathan teased.

At that moment, Senator Morton came into the room from the hallway, and Mrs. Taft opened her bedroom door and joined them.

"That was well timed," the senator said, smiling at Mandie's grandmother.

"Perfect," Mrs. Taft agreed.

Mrs. Taft and the senator led the way out of the room. They walked down several corridors before they came to the huge dining room. Mandie could smell the food, and she suddenly realized how hungry she was. She wondered what kind of a menu the Irish would have.

In the dining room, the waiter seated them in a corner by a window, which looked out onto the street in front of the hotel. Mandie was delighted that she could watch the pedestrians outside. On the other hand, she had to twist her neck to see the rest of the dining room.

"Grandmother, I need to take Snowball some food when we're finished," Mandie reminded Mrs. Taft. "Then I thought he could go with us on our walk and get some fresh air."

"Yes, dear." Her grandmother nodded, then looked

at the waiter who stood ready to take their order. "Let's hear what the hotel has to offer."

The waiter recited the list of food available, and Mandie listened in surprise. It sounded a lot like the fare of restaurants back home in North Carolina. Everyone ordered the ham with a variety of vegetables, and were delighted when the waiter placed a large bowl of biscuits on the table.

"I said I love Ireland. It's almost like back home," Mandie said as Mrs. Taft passed the biscuits to her.

"Remember, Amanda, a lot of the Irish immigrants in the early 1800s settled in our part of the country," Mrs. Taft explained. "They were among the first to leave their homes and travel to a foreign land. They found our part of the United States to be the most like their homeland. In fact, when you travel around Ireland you will see that even the landscape looks a lot like North Carolina's."

"I'm anxious to see everything," Mandie said as the waiter began placing the food before them. "What are we going to visit first?"

"There are lots of old castles, and a lot of old villages that haven't changed since their beginnings," Mrs. Taft told her.

The young people listened eagerly as they ate.

"There is an old, old linen mill here, too, that might be interesting," Senator Morton said.

"Yes, we must go there," Mrs. Taft agreed.

Mandie remembered the poster they'd seen. "Grandmother, there's a play here in Belfast right now called *Catch a Leprechaun*. Could we please go see it? Please?" Her blue eyes twinkled as she smiled at Mrs. Taft.

"A play about leprechauns? We'll see," her grandmother replied. "Senator Morton and I will plan our sightseeing schedule tonight."

Though Mandie wanted to see everything, the very word "sightseeing" sounded boring. The young people were tired of the usual sightseeing they did in every place they'd visited. They glanced at one another. Mandie knew her friends would endure most anything, if they could just see the play. Perhaps Uncle Ned could influence that. Her father's old Cherokee friend had joined them on their trip around Europe. He was presently visiting some acquaintances along the way and would catch up with them later.

Uncle Ned, who was not really Mandie's relative, had promised Jim Shaw, before he died, that he would watch over Mandie. Even though it meant crossing the big body of water between the United States and Europe, he had kept his promise. From time to time he showed up to check on Mandie.

As soon as they finished the meal, Mrs. Taft told Mandie she had fifteen minutes to take food to Snowball, then she was to bring him along for their walk around the town. Celia went with Mandie, and Jonathan stayed in the lobby with the adults.

"Hurry now, Snowball," Mandie told her cat as she watched him eat ham from the saucer she had brought to their room.

Celia was brushing her hair again in front of the mirror. "I'm not sure he understands you, Mandie," Celia said with a laugh.

"Oh, yes he does," Mandie said, looking at her friend. "You've been around Snowball long enough to know how intelligent he is, how much smarter than other cats." A sudden thought crossed her mind. "Maybe he can help us find a leprechaun!"

"Oh, Mandie, if there *is* such a thing as a leprechaun, it would probably frighten Snowball. They say cats are afraid of ghosts."

"Well, I wouldn't be afraid of a ghost if I ran across one," Mandie said, looking down at Snowball who had finished eating and was washing his face. "Let me just put on his leash, and we'll be ready." She crossed the room to retrieve the red leash from the bureau top.

"I'd like to see what you would do if you saw a ghost," Celia teased.

"What do you mean, what I would do?" Mandie said, looking up at her friend as she fastened Snowball's leash. "I'd like to see what *you* would do. You'd probably be frightened right out of your skin!"

Celia's face turned solemn. "You're right, I probably would be. I hope I never see a ghost, if there is such a thing."

"How about a leprechaun? Remember, you're going to help me find one," Mandie coaxed.

"Well, that's different," Celia said, "because we'll probably never see a leprechaun, either."

"I plan on finding one, Celia, if they do exist. I *will* find one, rest assured of that," Mandie stated, standing up. "Come on. Let's go."

The girls joined the others in the lobby, Mandie keeping Snowball in tow. Mrs. Taft and Senator Morton led the way outside. "You decide which way," Mrs. Taft told the senator. He was a tall man, distinguished-looking.

"If you insist," Senator Morton replied with a smile. "Let's take this slight hill to the right. If we take the upgrade while we're all fresh and anxious for a walk, then coming back we'll be going downhill when we're a little tired."

"Sounds like a good idea," Mrs. Taft assured him. Looking to the young people, she told them, "Now be sure to stay right behind us. We don't want to get separated. And, Amanda, please hold on to that cat."

"Yes, ma'am," Mandie replied as she gripped her fingers tighter around the end of the leash. Snowball pranced along, obviously enjoying the fresh air and the freedom to run now and then as he tugged at the leash, causing Mandie to walk faster.

Mrs. Taft enjoyed exploring all the shops along the way, and so did not keep a strict check on the young people. Senator Morton stayed with Mrs. Taft, and Mandie lagged behind with her friends when she spotted something unusual or interesting. Eventually Jonathan joined the adults, leaving the girls to themselves.

Mandie and Celia were out of hearing distance from the others, when suddenly a little girl came running across the street and almost fell on top of Snowball as she bent to look at him.

"Ah, 'tis a bea-you-tiful cat ye have, I say," the little girl said as she picked up Snowball while Mandie secured the end of the leash.

Mandie looked at the child more closely. She was about seven years old and was barefoot. Her dress, a faded blue, was soiled down the front. The girl pushed her carrot-red hair back from her small face with a dirty hand and stared up at Mandie with bright blue eyes.

"Where is your mother? Are you here on the street all alone?" Mandie asked.

"Me mither is workin'," the child replied, holding tightly to Snowball, who seemed to enjoy the loving pats she was giving him.

"Then shouldn't you be at home?" Mandie asked.

The child looked thoughtfully for a moment, and then said loudly, "Ah, ye be a foreigner, that ye be." She looked at Celia and asked, "Ye talk strange, too?"

Celia smiled at her and said, "We're from the United States. We're just visiting your country. What is your name?"

"Yawl came on the big boat then?" the child asked.

Mandie was surprised to hear the girl say "yawl," and asked, "Did you say y'all?"

"Sure'n I did. 'Tis Gaelic, y-a-w-l. We speak Gaelic in our house," she explained. "It means you and you."

"I understand," Mandie said, looking at Celia, who was also grasping the origin of the expression. "Back where we come from we say 'y'all,' but we spell it differently. It means *you all* in the United States. Our y'all must have originated here."

"Isn't that interesting!" Celia exclaimed. "Talk some more for us. You didn't tell us your name."

"When I was born me mither called me Molly, and that I still am," the child said.

"What are you doing out here on the street by yourself, Molly?" Mandie asked her.

" 'Tis a leprechaun I look for. Then me mither—" Molly began.

Mandie interrupted excitedly. "A leprechaun? Are you really looking for a leprechaun?"

Molly looked puzzled. " 'Tis only one I'm hoping to catch," she said.

"Why do you want to catch a leprechaun?" Celia asked.

Molly shook her head and said, "Ah, don't ye be knowin'? 'Tis not the leprechaun I want, 'tis his pot of gold. But first I must find the leprechaun."

"His pot of gold?" Mandie questioned.

"Ye don't be knowin' that every leprechaun has a pot of gold? If I can find just one leprechaun, and get his pot of gold, then me mither won't have to work so hard," Molly tried to explain as she continued to rub Snowball, who was purring loudly.

Tears came to Mandie's blue eyes as she realized how

poor the little girl and her mother must be. "Where does your mother work?" she asked.

Molly shrugged and said, "Everywhere. All day, all night. Mostly in the linen mill."

"And what does your father do? Where does he work?" Mandie asked.

Molly looked up at Mandie with sad eyes and said, "Me father is not in this world."

Mandie realized her father must be dead, and she said, "My father is not in this world, either."

Molly pointed ahead to Senator Morton and Mrs. Taft, who were within sight by an outdoor shop. "Then who be that man if he not be yer father?"

Mandie laughed and tried to explain. "That's Senator Morton. He's a good friend of my grandmother. That's my grandmother with him. My mother is back home in North Carolina—in the United States."

"I don't have a father, either," Celia commented.

Molly looked at her for a moment and then said, "Do ye be jokin'? Every one and all of us has a father."

Celia explained, "I mean he's dead, also; he's not in this world."

Molly nodded in understanding. "Then ye poor mither must work," she said. "Ye must find a leprechaun, too, and get his pot of gold."

Celia and Mandie looked at each other and smiled.

"We'll help you look for a leprechaun, if you'll tell us how," Mandie said. "And we don't want his pot of gold. You can have it."

"Ye will help me?" Molly asked with sparkling eyes. Then suddenly her face became sad. "But ye won't stay here long, and I can't go to America."

"Oh, but we will be here in Belfast for a few days. That

ought to be long enough to find a leprechaun, shouldn't it?" Mandie wondered aloud.

Molly shrugged and said, "Maybe. Sometimes one can be found soon, but sometimes it takes a long time."

"Have you found one before?" Celia asked.

"Sure. 'Tis three I have seen, but each time they get away," Molly said.

"With both of us helping you, it ought to be easier to catch one," Mandie encouraged.

"Maybe," Molly replied, rubbing her face against Snowball's white fur as she put him down.

"Look, we're staying at the Shamrock Inn. Do you know where that is, back that way?" Mandie pointed.

"That is the biggest and best place to stay in Belfast," Molly said, her blue eyes filled with wonder.

"Where do you live?" Mandie asked.

Molly pointed across the street and said, "Ye go that way, and then that way, and then the other way."

"What's the name of the street you live on?" Mandie asked.

"I don't be livin' in a street. I be livin' in a house," Molly declared.

"Of course. What is the name of the street that goes by your house?" Celia asked.

"Murphy Lane," Molly said.

"And does your house have a number on it? So the mailman knows where to deliver your mail?" Mandie asked.

Molly thought for a moment and then said, "There be a big number nine over the doorway."

Mandie told her, "We'll find you later then, Molly. We'll help you find a leprechaun."

" 'Tis grateful I would be, miss," Molly said and then asked, "What might yer name be?"

"Oh, I'm sorry. I'm Mandie Shaw, and this is my friend Celia Hamilton. My grandmother is Mrs. Taft," Mandie said as she looked toward the adults. "And that fellow you see coming this way is Jonathan Guyer. But we don't want him to help us find the leprechaun. Do you understand?"

"That I do," Molly said, watching the boy approach them.

The first thing Molly said when Jonathan had joined them, was, "Ye cannot help us find a leprechaun!"

Jonathan looked puzzled as he looked at Mandie and Celia. "Find a leprechaun?" he asked.

Mandie rolled her eyes, and Celia wouldn't look at him.

"She is looking for a leprechaun," Mandie said, tossing her head without looking directly at Jonathan. She took Snowball in her arms and said to Molly, "I hope you find the leprechaun. We'll see you later. Goodbye." Mandie started to walk away.

"That be the bargain," Molly said, waving to them as she ran back across the street.

"She believes in leprechauns?" Jonathan asked as the three began hurrying toward the adults.

"I suppose so, since she said she was looking for one," Mandie answered quickly. "Let's catch up with Grandmother and Senator Morton."

Jonathan kept pace with her and asked, "What did she mean, I couldn't help find a leprechaun?"

"I suppose she meant that you couldn't help find a leprechaun," Mandie said without looking at him.

"I believe she actually said, 'You cannot help *us* find a leprechaun.' Does that mean you are going to help her find one?" Jonathan asked with his mischievous grin.

Mandie stopped, planting her feet firmly on the

ground. "She wants to find a leprechaun and get his pot of gold for her mother, so she won't have to work so hard. That's it. Now let's drop the subject." She turned and stepped to her grandmother's side.

"Let's continue for another block," Mrs. Taft said, as Jonathan and Celia joined them. "Then we'll cross over and return on the other side of the street. By then we should all be sufficiently tired to go to bed after our long journey from Holland."

When they crossed the street to return to their hotel, Mandie glanced around, hoping to see Molly. But there was no sign of the child. She let Snowball down to walk at the end of his leash.

Mandie was deep in thought, and she paid no attention to the scenery along the way. All she could think of was Molly and her search for a leprechaun and his pot of gold. The child's obvious poverty had deeply touched Mandie, and she was trying to figure out what she could do to help. She also wondered if there really were such things as leprechauns in this country of Ireland.

At the door to the hotel, Mrs. Taft told the young people, "Amanda, you and Celia and Jonathan go to your rooms now and get ready for bed. The senator and I are going to have a cup of coffee in the dining room while we discuss plans for tomorrow."

"Yes, ma'am," the three chorused as they all entered the lobby.

"Be up and ready for breakfast at seven in the morning so we can get a good start on the day," Mrs. Taft added as she and the senator headed toward the dining room.

"Yes, ma'am," the three chorused again as they walked down the corridor to their rooms.

The girls said good-night to Jonathan and entered

their room. Mandie untied her bonnet and tossed it on the bureau, then kicked off her shoes as she flopped into a chair.

"Whew! I believe I am tired," she said with a sigh.

Celia began getting ready for bed and stopped to speak to her friend. "Don't get too comfortable in that chair. The sooner you get into bed the sooner you can get to sleep."

"You're right," Mandie agreed. She jumped up and quickly got out of her dress and into her nightgown. "I think part of my weariness comes from thinking about little Molly. Why, she may not even have enough to eat! They must be awfully poor."

"I was thinking the same thing," Celia said as she pulled her long nightgown over her head and jumped into bed.

"I'm more determined than ever to find a leprechaun," Mandie said as she crawled under the covers. "Can you imagine? A pot of gold! We could give it to Molly's mother."

"I'm afraid we could be looking forever for a leprechaun, Mandie," Celia told her.

"Well, it won't hurt to try," Mandie said. "And if we don't find one by the time we leave Ireland, I'll talk to Grandmother about Molly. Maybe she can help her in some way."

"I don't see how we're going to get away from Jonathan long enough to go looking for a leprechaun," Celia fretted.

"I'll figure out a way," Mandie assured her. "Maybe his father will come and get him while we're here in Ireland."

"His father doesn't seem too interested in coming after him, Mandie. You know Senator Morton wires him from wherever we are. He knows that Jonathan has been with us throughout Europe, but he always has some excuse for not catching up with Jonathan," Celia said.

Snowball jumped up onto the bed, circled a few times, then curled up at Mandie's feet.

"I know," Mandie said. "I feel sorry for Jonathan. Maybe his aunt and uncle will get back to their home in Paris, and he can stay there awhile. Anyhow, I'll figure out some way to keep Jonathan from knowing we're actually looking for a leprechaun."

"Good-night then," Celia said as she turned over to face the wall on her side of the bed.

"Good-night," Mandie murmured as she drifted off to sleep.

Chapter 3 / Sightseeing Surprise

The next morning brought a bright, sunshiny day. The dining room in the hotel was warm and cozy, and Mandie discovered that an Irish breakfast was a feast. She had always thought their housekeeper back home, Aunt Lou, served too much food—but the Irish had outdone her.

As everyone sat around the food-laden table, Mrs. Taft returned thanks and began passing the attractively prepared dishes.

Mandie set the bowl down that Jonathan had just handed her. "Grandmother, I just can't eat all this food!"

"Well, dear, they don't mean for us to eat everything on the table. Just partake of whatever you think you can consume. We don't want to waste the food," Mrs. Taft told her.

Her remark immediately reminded Mandie of Molly. Food was no doubt scarce at the child's home. Mandie wished she could have brought Molly here to eat. But she didn't mention her to her grandmother because she wanted to see what she could do to help Molly find a leprechaun.

"When we finish our breakfast, we'll go out to the linen mill and get on with our sightseeing," Mrs. Taft told the young people.

"What about the play, Grandmother?" Mandie asked. "Will we be able to see it?"

Jonathan and Celia stopped eating to hear the answer.

"We'll try to, dear," Mrs. Taft promised. "I'm not sure how far the theater is from here, though. Belfast is a good-sized city."

"It didn't seem large when we left the boat," Celia said as she continued eating.

"That's because our hotel is so near the wharf. We haven't been all the way into the heart of the city yet," Senator Morton told them.

"It's awfully old, isn't it?" Mandie said as she drank her coffee. So far, what she had seen of the town looked ancient.

"The city's charter was granted in 1613 by James I," Senator Morton explained. "So that's rather old, I'd say."

Mandie smiled at the handsome, white-haired senator. "You always know everything about all the places we visit," she said.

Senator Morton's eyes twinkled as he smiled and replied, "Oh, but that's because I gather information ahead of time on any place we're going to visit. I have traveled a lot in Europe myself, but I certainly don't know everything."

"I've been here a few times, too," Jonathan spoke up as he cut into a slice of ham. "In the schools I've been to in Europe we always studied about other cities and countries, and we visited the places we studied about."

Mandie looked at him and said, "You've been awfully lucky to be able to do all that."

Mrs. Taft, overhearing Mandie's remark, said, "You see, Amanda, you could do all those things, too, if you'd come to school here in Europe. I'll talk to your mother about it."

"Oh, no, Grandmother. I don't want to go to school over here. It's too far away. I wouldn't be able to see my mother very often," Mandie protested. "Even the school I go to in Asheville is too far from home."

"We'll see, dear. Now all of you eat up so we can be on our way," Mrs. Taft said, looking around the table.

Mandie knew what Celia was thinking. Mrs. Taft had also suggested, another time, that Celia go to school with Mandie in Europe. Celia didn't like the idea any more than Mandie did. And Mandie knew Jonathan was thinking of the way his father had sent him off to schools so far away that Jonathan never had a chance to stay home after his mother died. His father was wealthy and had so many business deals going on all over the world that he was seldom at home in New York.

Snowball's leash was tied to a table leg, and he had a saucer of food in front of him. That way he would be finished with his breakfast when Mandie was and could go with her. When her grandmother wasn't looking, Mandie added food to the kitten's saucer. The talk about going to school in Europe had completely ruined Mandie's appetite.

Finally, when they all were finished, they went out to a carriage Senator Morton had engaged for the day. Mandie was last through the front door of the hotel because Snowball was not cooperating at the end of his leash. When she stepped outside, Mandie was surprised to find Molly waiting for her. She was wearing the same dress, and didn't look as though she'd bathed either.

"Ye be ready to go huntin'?" the child asked eagerly.

Mandie immediately felt guilty for having eaten at a table overflowing with food while Molly sat out here, probably hungry. Then Mandie had a bright idea.

"No, I can't go right now. I have to go with my grandmother and the others," Mandie told her. "But you wait here. I'll be right back."

Celia overheard their conversation and said to Mandie under her breath, "Food?"

Mandie nodded. "Tell Grandmother I'll be back in a minute." She handed the end of Snowball's leash to Celia and rushed back inside the hotel.

Mandie went straight to the dining room and found to her relief that their table had not been cleared. The waiter, however, was approaching it just as she did.

"Just a minute, please," Mandie said politely, grabbing a cloth napkin and filling it with ham and sweet rolls. Everything else was too messy to carry in a napkin.

The waiter stood by watching and smiling. Mandie looked up at him and muttered, "I might get hungry later."

The waiter nodded and continued to smile as Mandie hurried out of the dining room.

Molly was still waiting in front of the hotel. Celia and Snowball had already boarded the vehicle with the others.

"Here, Molly, I thought you might like this," Mandie told the child as she handed the bulging napkin to her.

Molly took it and opened it. Her blue eyes grew round. "Be this for me? All for me?"

Mandie stooped down to embrace her and said, "Yes, all for you. I have to go now. I'll see you soon."

The child immediately began stuffing the food into her mouth. She only stopped long enough to wave good-bye to Mandie as she climbed into the carriage. Mandie felt her eyes fill with tears as she watched Molly from the window. Celia squeezed Mandie's hand. Jonathan looked at them both and then at the girl in front of the hotel.

Mrs. Taft and Senator Morton were deep into their own conversation. The young people were silent.

Their carriage turned into a narrow street, and Mandie noticed the swinging sign on the corner. It read "Murphy Lane."

"Look!" she whispered to Celia. "This is the street Molly lives on. Look for a number nine."

The girls watched for numbers, but the carriage was traveling too fast to scrutinize the cracked facades of the houses. The whole street looked impoverished.

Senator Morton began telling the young people what they were passing, along with the history of the area, but Mandie's mind was fixed on the way Molly devoured the food she had given her.

Finally they came to the old linen mill. It had stood there hundreds of years, according to Senator Morton, but was still in operation. The stone walls had only a few small windows, and lots of old trees grew around the building.

"How do they make linen?" Mandie asked as they stepped from the carriage.

The guard at the door would not allow them inside. He told Senator Morton that only the people who worked there were allowed to enter the building. The senator tried persuading him but to no avail.

"You probably know that flax grows in fields," Senator Morton began his explanation to Mandie. "Most of it has blue flowers in the spring. Fiber is stripped from the plant and is spun into thread, which is then woven into cloth."

"The seed of the plant, called flaxseed, is used for medicinal purposes," Mrs. Taft added.

Just then, Mandie glimpsed someone out of the corner of her eye. She snatched Snowball into her arms and ran to the end of the building. The strange woman they had seen on their voyage over was just rounding the far corner of the structure. Mandie looked back at her grandmother, trying to decide whether or not to pursue the woman. Her grandmother was shaking her head, and Mandie knew it was useless. The woman always managed to disappear anyway.

"Amanda, where are you going?" her grandmother called to her.

Mandie returned to the group gathered under the trees. "Nowhere, Grandmother," she said, smiling. "Nowhere."

Mrs. Taft turned to speak to Senator Morton, and Mandie quickly whispered to her friends, "I saw the strange woman from the ship!"

Jonathan's interest was immediately aroused. "You did? Why didn't you holler? One day we're going to catch her. Today might have been the day," he said in hushed tones.

"I wonder why that woman follows us everywhere we go?" Celia whispered. "Ever since we saw her on the ship coming to Europe she has turned up in every country we've visited."

The woman Mandie saw had traveled on the ship from the United States to England and had made various appearances. Occasionally, they were able to ask her questions, but she would never answer them directly. She always seemed to be fussing at them about something. Always dressed in black, she was small and old. The young people had begun to take for granted that she would show up wherever they went.

"Amanda," Mrs. Taft finally said, "all of you come on.

There is an old castle farther down the road that I want you to see."

"A real castle?" Mandie asked, genuinely curious.

"Of course a real castle," Mrs. Taft said as they all boarded the waiting carriage. "But no one lives there, Senator Morton says."

"This will be interesting," Celia remarked as they took their seats inside the vehicle.

"How old is it?" Jonathan asked the senator.

"Probably several hundred years," he said as the carriage moved down the road. "I visited there a long time ago. It was empty then, but seemed in pretty good shape for its age."

Soon the driver pulled the vehicle off the main road onto a narrow, bumpy lane.

"Oh, dear, do you suppose the driver is going the right way?" Mrs. Taft asked the senator.

"Yes, I remember the way. But the lane wasn't so rough the last time I was here," the senator told her. "I'm sorry."

"That's perfectly all right, Senator," Mrs. Taft said as the vehicle shook so hard her voice trembled. She held on to her seat with both hands.

Snowball didn't like the jolting, either, and began to meow and dig his claws into Mandie's shoulder.

Suddenly the bottom of the carriage seemed to catch on something and the vehicle abruptly stopped. The driver jumped out and appeared at the passenger door.

" 'Tis sorry that I be, sir, but we kinnot go another step. The road is impassable," he explained to Senator Morton.

"The carriage is stuck? It won't move at all?" the senator asked.

"Aye, sir. It can move backward but not forward," the man explained.

"Oh, dear," Mrs. Taft gasped. "Does that mean we must ride backwards all the way to the main road?"

"No, madam, I kin turn it 'round, but first ye must all alight," the driver told her.

"Let's get out then," Mrs. Taft stepped toward the door and the driver helped her from the carriage. The others followed. They all stood back out of the way and watched the driver maneuver the carriage.

"How much farther is this castle?" Mrs. Taft asked the senator.

"Maybe a hundred yards. If the trees weren't so thick, I'm sure we could see it from here," Senator Morton said.

"Then couldn't we walk ahead and look it over while the driver is turning the carriage around?" Mrs. Taft said as she looked down at her sensible shoes. "I did remember to wear my walking shoes today."

"Of course, if you wish. Let me just inform the driver," Senator Morton said as he walked toward the carriage, which was barely moving.

The young people waited with Mrs. Taft, and Celia remarked, "There sure are a lot of bad roads in the places we travel, aren't there?"

"Yes, and we can't always trust the driver," Mandie reminded them. "Remember the one in Germany who was a crook and wrecked the carriage and left us stranded?"

Celia gasped. "Do you think we can trust this driver? Will he wait for us while we walk on to the castle?"

Senator Morton returned to the group and overheard Celia's question. He smiled at her. "Don't worry about this driver. I haven't paid him yet. He won't run off and leave us."

"Shall we go on then?" Mrs. Taft asked.

"Yes. We'll just follow this lane; it will lead us right to the old castle," Senator Morton said, offering Mrs. Taft his arm. Mandie carried Snowball and followed with the others.

Jonathan walked behind Mandie and Celia on the narrow trail. "Who knows? Maybe we'll find a leprechaun down this old, deserted road."

Mandie glanced back at him. He was smiling, and she stopped in front of him. "Jonathan Guyer, I hope we do find a leprechaun. I imagine it would absolutely scare the daylights out of you."

"Maybe," Jonathan said with a shrug. "Only I don't think I have any daylights, whatever that is, in me."

"You know what I mean," Mandie said. "I hope one shows up before we leave Ireland, so when I go home I can at least say I saw a leprechaun."

"Mandie," Celia said, "your grandmother and the senator are almost out of sight around the curve ahead."

"And I don't want to lose them out here in this deserted place," Mandie said. As she walked along, Mandie thought about Molly and her pursuit of a leprechaun. She wondered how she could help her, and how she could do it without Jonathan. Mandie wasn't sure she even believed in leprechauns, but she did want to see what Molly was up to. The child seemed so certain about the little creatures and their pots of gold.

Maybe Uncle Ned will join us soon, Mandie thought. *He wasn't specific as to when he would catch up with us in Ireland. And he probably believes in leprechauns because Cherokee Indians believe in spirits.*

Suddenly the toe of Mandie's shoe caught on something, and she would have fallen flat on her face if Jonathan hadn't quickly caught her by the elbow. Snowball managed to jump free, and raced off down the trail after Mrs. Taft and Senator Morton, his red leash dragging behind him.

Mandie brushed her skirt off. "Thank you, Jonathan," she said. When she realized her cat was loose, she hurried after him, "Snowball! You come back here!"

Celia and Jonathan joined the chase, but by the time Snowball reached the adults, Senator Morton quickly stepped on the trailing leash, causing him to halt.

"Snowball, you naughty cat," Mandie said, scooping him into her arms.

"Amanda, please be more careful with that cat. He could have been lost in these trees," Mrs. Taft scolded.

"Yes, Grandmother," Mandie said. "I tripped." She looked back at Jonathan, suddenly remorseful about her teasing and speaking harshly to him. "I'm sorry for the way I've talked to you. Please forgive me."

"Forgive you? For what?" Jonathan said with his mischievous grin. "I thought that was your natural way of speaking."

"Forgive me, please?" Mandie solemnly asked again.

Jonathan just nodded his head. "Come on. Let's get going. We're being left behind again."

Mandie looked up the trail and saw that her grandmother and the senator were nearing the castle. She walked faster, but this time watched her step more carefully.

When the old castle came into full view, the young people stopped to stare at the stone structure. It was huge and seemed to expand on into the woods.

"Let's go inside!" Mandie said, noticing Mrs. Taft and Senator Morton walking around one end of it.

"How do we get inside?" Celia asked. "I don't see any door."

Mandie searched the front of the building for a door. There didn't seem to be one, at least not in plain sight. Her attention was drawn to an upstairs window, and to her amazement, she saw that the strange woman from the ship was watching them.

"Look, there's that woman!" Mandie pushed her two friends. "Come on!" she exclaimed, running ahead.

Mandie turned the corner and found a huge archway into the building. "Come on, I've found an entrance!"

Once inside, the three looked around, at a loss as to how to get to the upper floors. There didn't seem to be any stairs. The place was a maze of huge rooms, and they soon became disoriented. They couldn't even find the way back to the archway where they had entered.

Mandie stopped suddenly. "We've got to at least get back outside. Grandmother and Senator Morton don't know where we are."

"There must be some way to get upstairs. That strange woman didn't just fly up there," Jonathan said as he continued to look around.

All at once they heard a loud scraping noise, and quickly searched for the source of the sound. Mandie turned just in time to see the strange woman replacing a large stone as she stepped into a nearby room.

"Wait!" Mandie called to her.

The woman whirled and disappeared again. Mandie, with Celia and Jonathan right behind her, stopped to investigate the large stone. Mandie gave it a push. It moved, revealing an opening and what looked like a stone staircase.

"Look! A secret stairwell!" Mandie exclaimed.

"Well, what do you know," Jonathan said with a smile.

"We aren't going up those dark steps, are we?" Celia asked nervously.

Not answering Celia, Mandie said, "We probably could have caught the woman if we'd tried, but I suppose she's gone by now. Let's go on up the stairs," Mandie said, looking at Jonathan.

"Whatever you say," he answered, shrugging.

"Do we have to?" Celia asked, biting her lips.

"Here, give me your hand," Jonathan told her. "That woman was up there. You'll be safe."

"Come on," Mandie said, leading the way. She held Snowball tightly in one arm while she used her other hand to grope for a handrail. There was none, and the wall was slippery. She moved up with caution.

The stairwell was circular, and when Mandie arrived at the top she found herself in a huge room with an open fireplace. She went to the window where the woman had apparently stood, and saw her grandmother and the senator below.

"Amanda, where are you?" Mrs. Taft was calling.

"I'm up here, Grandmother," Mandie called down to her.

Mrs. Taft looked up. "Oh, dear, Amanda. Y'all come down here right now."

"We'll be right down, Grandmother," Mandie said, turning back to her friends. "Guess we'd better go down."

The three slowly made their way back down the dark stairs and carefully replaced the stone. They hurried out into the yard and found Mrs. Taft and Senator Morton waiting for them in the same spot.

"I was afraid to move for fear y'all would not find us," Mrs. Taft said as she took a deep breath. "Amanda, y'all shouldn't ever run off in such a strange, isolated place. Now let's get back to the carriage."

Yes, ma'am," the three chorused as they followed the adults down the trail.

When they arrived at the carriage, the driver was sitting on a log in the shade waiting for them.

"Thank goodness, he didn't leave us!" Mrs. Taft said with a sigh of relief.

"I told you he wouldn't leave," Senator Morton reminded her.

The young people looked at one another and laughed. "So Grandmother was thinking the same thing we were," Mandie muttered.

"I wonder if your grandmother or the senator saw the strange woman," Celia remarked quietly.

"I don't think so," Mandie said. "They would have said something about it. Even if they didn't recognize her, I'm sure they would have mentioned seeing anyone in a deserted place like this."

They all climbed back into the carriage and were off for more sightseeing. Mandie settled down in her seat and her thoughts returned to Molly. She wished they would go back to the hotel soon. Now that she knew where Molly lived, she could go find her.

And it would be interesting to see where Molly would take her and Celia in her search for a leprechaun.

Chapter 4 / Revealing Information

The streets of Belfast were cobblestoned and narrow, winding up and down hills and around curves. Maybe it was Mandie's always-ready smile or her twinkling blue eyes, but she never met a stranger who wasn't willing to share a conversation. Everyone was friendly and talkative here.

After a quick bite to eat at noon at an outdoor cafe, Mrs. Taft, as always, insisted on visiting a museum. The three young people moaned together when they heard it. Mandie didn't know much about art, and she was more interested in watching and meeting people.

Their carriage pulled up in front of a huge, stone structure amid blooming flowers, shrubbery, trees, and green, green grass in a park. Walkways wound around the building and out of sight. A magnificent fountain sent a fine spray of water cascading down in the bright sunlight.

"At least it is a beautiful place!" Mandie exclaimed as

she followed her grandmother out of the vehicle.

Mrs. Taft glanced back at her and said, "Amanda, you will have to leave Snowball out here. I don't think he will be allowed inside."

Mandie looked around and asked, "But where, Grandmother? Where can I leave him?"

"Just tie his leash to the seat in the carriage. He'll be all right. Our driver will watch him," Mrs. Taft told her.

Mrs. Taft walked up to the building with Senator Morton while Jonathan and Celia waited for Mandie.

Mandie turned to speak to the driver. "My grandmother says I have to leave my cat inside the carriage. Will you watch him for me?"

" 'Tis that I will, miss," the tall man assured her as he stood beside the horses.

"Thank you." Mandie entered the vehicle and carefully looped Snowball's red leash through the open arm of the seat. "You stay here now, Snowball, and don't try to get loose and run away, you hear? I won't be gone long. I'm not too interested in this place." She patted him on the head.

Worried about leaving her cat alone, Mandie spoke to the driver again, "He's tied to the seat, but I'd appreciate it if you would keep an eye on him for me." She smiled up at the man.

"Of course, miss. I'll be sure he's all right," the driver promised.

Mandie joined her friends, and the three entered the building to find Mrs. Taft and Senator Morton waiting for them at the front entrance.

"I sure hope Snowball doesn't get loose and run away," Mandie said with a sigh.

"Oh, he'll be all right with the driver there watching him," Jonathan assured her.

"And the driver looks like a nice man. He did wait for us at the castle, remember." Celia tried to sound encouraging.

"And Senator Morton still hasn't paid him. I heard him tell the driver he would settle up with him when we return to the hotel. So don't worry. Just enjoy this great museum," Jonathan said with a grin.

Mandie started to tell her friends what she really thought of museums when Mrs. Taft called to them to hurry along.

The three young people joined the adults and soon found themselves in a wide hallway with other sightseers. Archways opened on either side of the corridor, leading to rooms full of paintings. Elaborate draperies covered the high walls.

Mrs. Taft and Senator Morton stopped at the first room, and Mrs. Taft said, "I suppose we should just begin with the first one and keep moving forward until we have seen everything."

"That sounds reasonable to me," Senator Morton agreed.

Looking back at the young people, Mrs. Taft admonished them, "Now I want you all to stay close together. We don't want to have to go looking for any of you. Is that clear?"

"Yes, ma'am," the three chorused. When Mrs. Taft turned back to the senator, the young people exchanged sighs.

"No chance to explore on our own, I guess," Mandie moaned.

"We'd better not, Mandie," Celia warned. "Not this time."

"It depends on what we run into," Jonathan said with his mischievous grin.

The three followed the adults into the first room to the right. The walls were covered with paintings, and more paintings were displayed on tables around the room. Mandie watched as her grandmother and the senator looked at one painting after another with obvious interest.

"Do y'all really think this huge building contains nothing but paintings?" Mandie asked Celia and Jonathan.

Jonathan raised his dark eyebrows as he replied, "That would be an awful lot of them, if that's all there is in this museum."

Mandie glanced around the room at the paintings she could see between the sightseers. "It looks like every painting in this room is a water scene."

Jonathan agreed. "It does look that way."

"I can't see them all, with all these people in here, but the ones I can see are definitely paintings of water," Celia said.

"I wonder what's in the next room?" Mandie said, motioning for her friends to follow her. Her grandmother and the senator were deeply absorbed with a painting. "Let's just take a peek." She slipped out through the archway and walked toward the next room. Celia and Jonathan followed.

"Mandie, ought we to be doing this?" Celia asked.

"Sh-h-h-h!" Mandie whispered. "We'll just look and then go back."

The three stopped at the entrance to the next room and looked inside. The paintings seemed to be of houses and buildings.

"This sure is an odd way to set up a museum," Mandie whispered to her friends as they gazed about the room. "All the museums I've ever been to had all kinds of paintings mixed together in a room."

"All the museums you've been to?" Jonathan teased. "How many is that? Let's see, we started out in Paris, and—"

"Well, even if I haven't been to any but the ones on this journey through Europe, I know it's been quite a few," Mandie interrupted.

"And that makes you an expert on how a museum should be laid out?" Jonathan asked.

Mandie stamped her foot. "Jonathan Guyer, I don't give a hoot what you say, I think it's unusual."

"I agree," Celia said, defending her friend.

At that moment, Mrs. Taft and Senator Morton emerged from the first room and walked toward them.

"Oh, there y'all are," Mrs. Taft said, smiling. "I suppose you're anxious to see everything. Well, don't get too far away from us."

Mandie and her friends sighed with relief as the two returned to the first room with the water scenes, leaving them at the doorway to the second room.

"Let's see what's in the next room," Mandie whispered. She led the way and stopped in the archway to stare inside.

Celia and Jonathan followed. "All portraits of people!" Celia exclaimed.

"Yes, as far as I can see," Mandie said. "Let's just look inside each room to see what's there, and then come back here to catch up with Grandmother and Senator Morton."

The three moved together to the next room and found only paintings of flowers. That was the last room on the right. Straight ahead, at the end of the corridor, was a room with a set of double doors, where sightseers were going in and out.

"Maybe we'll find something different in there," Mandie said, pointing to the end of the hallway. "Let's see."

She hurried ahead, with Celia and Jonathan right behind her. The huge doors were heavy, and Jonathan reached to help Mandie open one of them. The three stepped inside a room that had writing and pictures painted directly on the walls. Mandie whirled around and was excited to see a statue standing in the middle of the floor. "Look! Look!" she exclaimed, walking around the statue. "It's a leprechaun!"

"Yes, Mandie, and I think the writing on the walls is all about leprechauns," Celia said, pointing to the script.

"This I've got to see," Jonathan said, moving closer to the wall in front of him.

"It *is* about leprechauns!" Mandie declared. "There really are such creatures. It says, 'Leprechauns are descended from the Tuatha De Danann.'" She read ahead quickly and then summarized aloud: "This race of warriors, who were all good people, lived in Ireland before the Celts. And they were invaded and defeated by Fomorian invaders led by Balor of the Evil Eye. Then it says the defeated Tuatha De Danann were forced to live underground by their conqueror. And this caused them to come back out years and years afterward as dwarfs—"

Jonathan interrupted as he read over her shoulder, "But this is all Irish myth and legend, Mandie. It's like a fairy tale—"

"'Tis no fairy tale," a loud voice spoke behind them.

The three young people turned to come face-to-face with a giant of a man who was wearing a green suit.

Mandie gasped and said, "Oh, no, of course it's not a fairy tale," although she couldn't figure out why she suddenly felt afraid of the tall, stout man.

"'Tis ye, lad, I be speakin' to," the man said, looking at Jonathan.

The girls had never seen Jonathan so completely at a loss for words. "I—er—I—ah, was just saying . . ." Jonathan stammered as he looked up at the stranger. "I—ah—was teasing the girls, sir."

"Jon-a-than!" Mandie exclaimed.

" 'Tis no teasin' matter, me lad," the man told the boy. "Or the statue wouldn't be in this fine place, now would it."

Celia spoke to Mandie, "We'd better be looking for your grandmother, don't you think?"

Jonathan swallowed hard and told the man, "I'm sorry, sir. I apologize. You see, we're from the United States and we don't believe—that is, we don't have leprechauns there."

The man bent slightly to shake a finger in Jonathan's face. "This is not America. This be Ireland. Ye must show respect for our history. How would ye like it iffen I went to your country and ridiculed your beliefs?"

Jonathan became agitated and quickly held out his hand, saying, "I apologize, sir. Please forgive me. I'm really and truly sorry."

The man straightened up, threw back his shoulders and said, "So this be how people in United States behave. Pity on me poor kin who went to live in your country. Humpf!" The man turned abruptly and left the room.

The young people looked at one another.

"Jonathan Guyer, let that be a lesson to you. You should practice what you preach. You told us not to let the Irish people know we didn't believe in leprechauns, and here you are embarrassing all of us," Mandie said. She stamped her foot and tossed her blonde hair so that her bonnet threatened to fall off.

"I'm sorry, Mandie. I didn't know there was anyone around to hear," Jonathan said.

"I'm going to find my grandmother!" Mandie said. She turned on her heels and left the room. Celia followed her, and Jonathan lagged slowly behind them.

Mandie found her grandmother and Senator Morton in the next room, deep in discussion of a painting. She told Celia, "Let's just wait at the doorway for them. They'll see us when they're ready to leave."

When Jonathan quietly joined them, Mandie ignored him. Celia stared at the floor, and Jonathan walked around in circles with his hands in his pockets.

When Mrs. Taft and Senator Morton finally turned to leave, Mandie told them, "The next room is the most interesting of all."

"It is? How do you know, dear?" Mrs. Taft asked.

"Because we went to look inside," Mandie replied. Leading the way, she added, "Come on, Grandmother. I'm sure you will like it."

Mrs. Taft and the senator looked at each other and followed the girls to the next room. Jonathan trailed sheepishly behind.

When Mandie pushed the door open, Mrs. Taft immediately noticed the leprechaun statue and went to examine it. "Why, it's almost real!"

Mandie excitedly told her grandmother to read the writing on the walls. "The walls tell the story of the leprechauns." She pointed to the large script.

"Don't forget we are part Irish," Mrs. Taft said. "I well remember my grandmother telling my sister and me about leprechauns when we were too young to read." She stopped talking long enough to read the words on the wall. "It's exactly what my grandmother told us many, many years ago."

Mandie was surprised that her grandmother knew so much about leprechauns. When she turned away from reading, Mandie asked, "Grandmother, do you believe in leprechauns?" She held her breath waiting for her answer.

Mrs. Taft looked at her in surprise. "Why, of course, dear. They are part of Ireland's history. Just as the story on the wall says."

"You really do believe in them?" Mandie asked, excited about her grandmother's reply. "Do you think we might see one while we're in Ireland?"

"Oh, Amanda," Mrs. Taft said with a smile. "I don't know that there are any leprechauns around nowadays. I'd put them in a category with the spirits that your Cherokee kinpeople believe in; something so mysterious that it is hard to prove one way or the other."

Mandie sighed disappointedly. "You know, Grandmother, some of these people here in Ireland believe there are such creatures now and claim to have seen them." She was thinking of Molly, who said she had seen leprechauns at least three times.

"I wouldn't count on seeing one, Amanda. You might be disappointed," Mrs. Taft said. "Now let's go on to the next room."

Mrs. Taft and Senator Morton led the way. They found a display of artifacts depicting the progress of Ireland. Tools, clothes, utensils, jewelry, and furniture were displayed in sealed glass cases.

"Apparently this museum is not just an art museum," Mandie remarked as they viewed the room.

"No, dear, this museum contains the culture of Ireland—the past and the present," Mrs. Taft explained. "Did you notice how old some of the paintings were? Others have been done more recently by artists who are still painting. This is a wonderful way to learn about Ireland."

"Yes, Grandmother," Mandie agreed as she stooped to look at the shoes displayed. Some of them were so old they were nothing but rags and strings. Looking up, she saw that the dresses were also old and threadbare.

"I'm glad we don't dress like that now," Celia remarked, pointing to a heavy gown with ruffles, lace, and a train. "I'd never be ready for anything on time."

"Neither would I," Mandie said with a laugh. "And look at the men's clothes." Turning, she looked for Jonathan, who was still moping. "Look, Jonathan. What if you had to wear that fancy suit of clothes?" She pointed to a velvet suit that looked old enough for George Washington to have worn it.

Jonathan slowly joined them to look in the cases. "I don't think I'd be comfortable in that at all. And just think of all the time and trouble to get it on. No, I think I like our clothes now much better."

"And a hundred years from now people will be looking at our clothes in a case like this and saying the same things we're saying about these," Mandie told her friends. "I wonder what the world will be wearing a hundred years from now."

"I guess I'll never know. I'd be too old to be living," Jonathan said with a slight smile.

"We'll probably all be gone by then," Celia added.

Mrs. Taft called to them across the room, "Let's move on. The day is leaving us."

The adults quickly moved on through the rest of the museum and finally decided to leave. Jonathan hadn't said another word to anyone. Mandie was feeling guilty for her outburst, and she purposely lagged behind to speak to him. Celia, seeming to understand what Mandie was doing, walked ahead with Mrs. Taft and Senator Morton.

"Jonathan, I have something to say to you," Mandie said, grabbing his sleeve.

Jonathan stopped and raised his eyebrows. "Well, what is it?" he asked.

Mandie cleared her throat, and looking straight into Jonathan's brown eyes, she said, "Jonathan, I'm sorry I got angry with you about the leprechauns. Will you forgive me, please?"

Jonathan shuffled his feet as his mischievous grin slowly spread across his face. "Oh, Mandie, you're always asking to be forgiven for something that doesn't amount to peanuts. You don't have to ask forgiveness. I'm the one who was wrong and I'm sorry," he said.

"Well, anyway, I'm sorry too," Mandie told him.

"Amanda, come on and get this cat," Mrs. Taft called to her as she stood at the door of the carriage.

"Oh, Snowball! I'd almost forgotten him!" Mandie said, running to the carriage.

Snowball had managed to cross over to Mrs. Taft's seat, and his tangled leash held him immobile.

The driver was talking to Mandie as she worked on the leash. "I'm sorry, miss. I figured since he couldn't get loose he'd be all right."

"Oh, he's all right, thank you. It's just that my grandmother can't sit down until I get him out of her seat," Mandie said, and with one final pull had the leash free. She picked up the white cat and said, "There now. I'll let you out to walk the next time we stop." She took her seat and cuddled Snowball in her lap.

"The next stop will be our hotel, dear," Mrs. Taft said as she sat down. "I think we all need a rest before suppertime and a chance to get freshened up."

Mandie immediately thought of Molly. Maybe she could find the little girl while her grandmother was resting. And Jonathan would think she was in her room, and she hoped Celia would go with her.

Mandie glanced at Celia and smiled at her before she said, "Yes, I do need some time to hang up some of my clothes; don't you, Jonathan? You said you couldn't find clothes that matched."

"I sure do. It'll be a relief to get my pants and jackets sorted out," Jonathan agreed.

When they arrived at the hotel, Mandie quickly glanced around outside for Molly, but there was no sign of the little girl. Mrs. Taft led the way through the lobby and on to their rooms.

With a final request that the girls be ready for supper in about an hour and a half, Mrs. Taft went into her room and closed the door.

Mandie smiled at Celia as she put Snowball down and took off his leash. "We have time to go out and look for Molly!" she said.

"We do?" Celia questioned as she sat down.

"Plenty of time. And I promise we'll be back in time to change clothes for supper," Mandie said as she stood up and straightened her skirts.

"Well, if you say so, Mandie," Celia reluctantly agreed.

"Come on. Let's go," Mandie said, opening the door to the hallway.

Now, if they could only get out of the hotel without Jonathan seeing them.

Chapter 5 / Number Nine, Murphy Lane

Mandie peeked out into the corridor and was just about to step outside their room when she saw the door to Jonathan's room slowly open. She stepped back, bumping into Celia as she pushed the door closed, leaving a tiny crack to peer through. She watched as Jonathan passed by.

"Sh-h-h-h!" Mandie warned Celia as she eased their door open farther so she could see where Jonathan was going. He disappeared around a corner of the hallway in the direction of the lobby.

"Shucks!" Mandie exclaimed, softly closing the door in order not to disturb her grandmother behind the closed door of her bedroom. "I wonder what Jonathan is up to."

"He's probably going outside," Celia said.

"Right. And if we could just find a rear entrance we could leave that way without running into him," Mandie told her, smiling thoughtfully.

"Let's look for one," Celia suggested.

"Let's go," Mandie agreed as the two girls softly slipped out into the corridor and began walking in the opposite direction from the front of the building.

They passed several closed doors, and then the hallway turned to the left. There were more closed doors, and the corridor angled to the right. There was lots of noise in this wing, and Mandie realized they must be near the kitchen. Laughter and talking could be heard over the rattle of dishes and pots and pans. And the air was filled with the aroma of good food.

"M-m-m-m, I think I'm hungry," Mandie said with a groan.

"Everything smells so good it makes me think I'm hungry, too," Celia agreed.

Mandie could see several open doors ahead along the corridor, and she slowed down to inspect each room as they passed. One big room looked like it stretched the length of the hallway, and Mandie could see uniformed workers scurrying about, preparing food in large pots, stacking dishes, and performing the many tasks required in a hotel kitchen.

As Mandie slowed down to look inside, Celia urged, "Let's not stop, Mandie. We don't have time, and besides, people will wonder what we're doing down here."

"But we need to find the back door, Celia," Mandie said, "and it might be in the kitchen." Just then she spotted a door on the far side of the room. When someone entered it she caught a glimpse of the outside. They would have to walk all the way across the kitchen to get to it.

Celia said with a sigh, "Oh, Mandie, we're not going in there through all those people, are we?"

"It's the only way to get to the back door. Just follow me. We can smile our way through," Mandie said, bracing her shoulders, slightly tilting her bonnet-covered head, and stepping into the big room.

The kitchen workers saw the girls and smiled and waved as they greeted them.

"We just want to use the back door," Mandie said quickly as she and Celia hurried toward it.

A tall, robust woman smiled and said, "But, lass, ye will find another door on down the hall, without soilin' ye fine dress."

By that time the girls were at the door and Mandie pulled it open. "Thank you, ma'am," Mandie said to the woman. "We'll try to find our way back in through the other door."

The girls stepped out into the yard, which was surrounded by a high wall. "Oh, I see the door the woman was referring to," Mandie said, pointing to the right. "There. See the tables and chairs outside?"

Celia looked, then gasped. "Yes, and I see Jonathan sitting at one of the tables, Mandie!"

Mandie saw him at the same time, and pulled Celia by the hand back toward the kitchen. Mandie said, "Come on. We'll just have to go back through here."

The workers appeared surprised to see the girls back so soon.

"We've decided to go out the front door," Mandie explained as she and Celia hurried through the busy kitchen and into the corridor.

"Whew!" Mandie said, stopping for a breath. "Now that we know where Jonathan is, we can just go out the front door and not worry about running into him. Come on. It'll be easier to find Molly's street from the front anyway."

The girls hurried back through the corridor and eventually came to the lobby. They stepped outside the front door and looked around.

"I don't see Molly anywhere," Mandie said. "We'll just have to walk toward her house. Maybe she's at home. I hope so." She led the way across the street toward Murphy Lane.

The houses on Murphy Lane looked average, but as the girls walked down the street, they noticed that the dwellings became more decrepit, with an occasional shop sandwiched here and there. Mandie watched for a number nine, but they had walked several blocks before they saw a house number that was even legible.

"Look," Mandie said. "That's number one hundred. I wonder which way the numbers get smaller, back the way we came or on ahead. What do you think?"

"I have no idea, Mandie," Celia replied. "All the houses are so old and dilapidated, I don't see how people can live in them. I'd be afraid the house would fall in on top of me."

"People may not live in all the houses on this street," Mandie suggested. "Some of them look vacant."

A few people passed the girls on the street, but otherwise the neighborhood looked isolated. They had not seen anyone hanging out clothes, digging in the yard, or even sitting outdoors, as they had seen in other areas.

"Maybe Molly didn't get it straight when she gave us her address," Celia said. "Do you suppose she meant that you go down this street to get to the street where she lives?"

"Maybe, but let's just walk on a little farther and see if we can find another house number," Mandie said.

When they could see Murphy Lane ending at a cross street ahead, Mandie suddenly spotted a number nine on the crumbling facade of an old stone house across the street. "There! There it is!" Mandie said, pointing excitedly. "Let's go knock on the door."

The front door was falling off its hinges and was only partially closed. The two windows on each side had no curtains and were so dirty it was impossible to see inside.

"Mandie, this is a terrible-looking place. Do you suppose Molly really lives here?" Celia asked.

"Let's find out," Mandie said. She couldn't decide whether to knock or just push the door open. She couldn't hear any noise inside. Maybe no one was home. She decided to knock, and if no one answered, she'd just push the door open and go in.

Celia waited while Mandie knocked hard several times on the rickety door, with no response from inside.

Mandie turned to Celia and said, "I'm going inside to see what's in here."

Before Celia could protest, Mandie gave the door a hard shove, and it moved inward enough to allow them to slip through. The light inside was dim, and Mandie had to wait until her eyes adjusted. Gradually she made out the interior of a front room and then a hallway.

"Mandie, let's not go any farther," Celia protested behind her. "We can't see anything."

"But I can tell the doors along the hallway are all open," Mandie said. "Come on."

Celia didn't budge. Mandie looked into the first room. There was nothing inside but a pile of old newspapers, rags, and debris. She moved on to the next one. It contained more of the same thing. She quickly checked each room and then returned to Celia in the front room. There was nothing but garbage everywhere.

"It's obvious that no one lives here," Mandie said to Celia. "It's deserted. I wonder why Molly gave us this address?"

Suddenly, a noise caught Mandie's attention. It sounded like someone was moving things around in a room toward the back of the house. Without stopping to think, Mandie hurried to investigate, following the sound as she went. She stepped into the room to look around. Unlike the others, it was very dark. Before she could see anything, strong hands grabbed her shoulders from behind.

"Let go of me!" she demanded, trying to pull free.

"Mandie!" Celia cried, rushing to help. She kicked at the man's legs.

"Help!" Mandie called at the top of her lungs. "Help! Celia, get help!" She tried to hit the man with her bag but couldn't swing her arms.

Celia ran out of the room, and the man tried to trip her with his foot. She rushed through the front door of the house, screaming, "Help!"

Before Mandie could wonder how long it would be before she would be rescued, Jonathan came rushing into the house with Celia and followed her to the room, where he began kicking the man. When that didn't loosen his grip, Jonathan grabbed a board lying in a trash pile and swung it with all his might at the man's head. Mandie felt the large hands release her as the man fell with a thud to the floor.

"Jonathan! You didn't kill him, did you?" Mandie exclaimed, looking at the huge man lying prostrate at their feet. She rotated her neck in an effort to relieve the pain.

"No, of course not," Jonathan said with a little laugh. "But do you realize you could have been killed?"

Mandie shivered at the thought. "Thank you, Jonathan. Thank you with all my heart. You saved my life."

"The man smells like whiskey. He must be drunk," Jonathan observed, "otherwise he wouldn't have fallen so easily. I'm sure he'll be all right. He'll just sleep it off."

"Oh, Jonathan, I want to thank you, too," Celia said

with a small whimper. "I don't know how Mandie could have gotten away from him."

Jonathan smiled and looked around as they walked toward the front door. "What are you girls doing in a dump like this anyway?"

Ignoring his question, Mandie asked, "How did you know where we were?"

"I'm a mind reader," he joked as they stepped out into the street.

"When I went out the front door for help," Celia explained, "Jonathan was headed straight for the house, and I almost bumped into him."

"But, Jonathan, how did you know where we were?" Mandie asked again.

Jonathan paused under a tree by the road, and the girls stopped to listen. "Well, I know that whenever Mrs. Taft says there's time for a rest, you girls manage to get into some kind of mischief," Jonathan began. "I walked around the hotel and couldn't see you anywhere, so I sat down at a table in the outdoor restaurant at the back. Then I saw you come out the kitchen door and then go back inside. I said to myself, 'Uh-huh, they are up to something.' So I rushed around to the front of the hotel in time to see you go off down this dirty old street, and then I really got worried. This is no neighborhood for two girls to be wandering around in without an escort."

"Thank goodness you saw us, Jonathan," Mandie told him as they walked back up Murphy Lane toward the hotel. "I have to make a confession."

"Oh no, I don't want to hear another confession," Jonathan groaned teasingly.

"Well, you're going to hear it anyway. You see, you teased me so much about leprechauns that I didn't want you to know what we were doing—" Mandie began.

Jonathan interrupted. "You've been out chasing leprechauns?" His dark eyes were wide with surprise.

"No, not exactly," Mandie said. "Remember the little girl, Molly, that we met on the street yesterday?"

"Sure, I remember her. She said I couldn't help you hunt for leprechauns," Jonathan replied. "Is that what you were doing?"

"I told you, no," Mandie said as the three walked on up the street. "We were actually looking for Molly. She said she lived at number nine Murphy Lane, and that's the address of the house we were in. But we couldn't find anyone there, except that old drunk, of course."

"My goodness!" Jonathan exclaimed. "You didn't believe anything that little ragamuffin said, did you?"

"Jonathan, Molly is not a ragamuffin. She's a little poor girl whose mother works in the linen mill," Mandie told him.

"And her father is dead," Celia added as they walked along.

"Why were you looking for her?" Jonathan asked.

"Because she said we could help her hunt leprechauns—" Mandie began.

With a howl of laughter Jonathan interrupted, "That's what I said. You were going out to look for leprechauns!"

"We merely wanted to see what Molly was doing first," Mandie quickly told him. "She told us she has seen three leprechauns, but they all got away. Well, I have a right to satisfy my own curiosity, so I decided I would find out how she went about finding them."

"All right, all right, I won't tease you anymore, I promise. But may I come with you next time?" Jonathan asked seriously.

"You really want to go looking for leprechauns?" Mandie asked. "That's a big switch. First you say you don't believe in them, and now you want to look for them."

"Actually, I want to go along to keep you girls out of trouble," Jonathan protested. "But who knows, if Molly knows where to find a leprechaun, I'd like to be there when she does."

"And you won't scare him away, or laugh at us?" Celia asked.

"Of course not. I said I wouldn't tease you anymore," Jonathan reminded her.

"All right then. I suppose you can go along, provided you don't make fun of us," Mandie decided as they neared the front door of the hotel.

"When are you girls going hunting, then?" Jonathan asked as he held the door open for them.

"You know how busy Grandmother keeps us. We'll just have to try the next time we get a chance," Mandie said as the three continued down the corridor toward their rooms. "But we have to find Molly first. We can't do anything without her."

"All right, I'll help you keep an eye out for her. See you both at supper," Jonathan said.

"We don't have much time to get dressed for supper," Celia reminded Mandie as they entered their bedroom and closed the door.

The girls quickly washed up and changed into clean clothes as they talked. Snowball was curled up in the middle of the big bed, asleep.

"I think I learned a lesson from that outing down Murphy Lane," Mandie said as she pulled on a blue voile dress. "I won't ever go into a neighborhood like that again without someone to protect us. I was scared almost to death. It was a horrible feeling."

"Me too," Celia agreed. "We should never go out alone in a strange country. I'm glad you told Jonathan he could accompany us next time."

"But if he begins teasing us again I won't put up with it," Mandie told her. She went to stand before the mirror and brush her long blonde hair.

"He said he wouldn't," Celia said. "I think Jonathan usually keeps his word." She joined Mandie at the looking glass. Her auburn curls were a mass of tangles.

"You know, I was wishing Grandmother would just pack up and we could go home soon, but now that we've gotten interested in leprechauns, I'd like to stay until we find one," Mandie said.

"I know how you feel about going home. I miss my mother. We've been gone ever since school was out and haven't had any time at home," Celia remarked as she tied a ribbon around her curls to match her white dress.

"I know. Just as soon as we get back home we're going to have to go to Asheville to school," Mandie said as she tied her hair back at the neck with a blue ribbon. She turned suddenly to Celia and said, "I sure hope Grandmother doesn't mention anything to my mother about sending me to school over here in Europe. I hope she just forgets about it."

"So do I," Celia said. "I don't want to go to a European school, and I don't think my mother would make me, but I don't want your mother to send you off either," Celia said. "Mandie, I wonder if Molly goes to school. Do you think she is old enough?"

"I suppose so. I don't know anything about the schools here in Ireland, but I imagine Molly is about seven years old, and back home she would already be in the second grade," Mandie replied as she turned before the full-length mirror to inspect herself. "I wonder where she lives. I don't see how anyone could live in that old trashy place we went into, do you?"

"Well, you hear things about people who are so poor they live on the street, but Molly said her mother works in the linen mill, so they must have a home somewhere," Celia said as she sat down on the side of the bed.

"Grandmother didn't say where we were going to eat supper tonight. I suppose in the hotel, but maybe some-place else. If we go out, Celia, will you help me watch for Molly?" Mandie asked as she joined Celia on the side of the bed. "I want to ask her some questions."

"Sure, Mandie," Celia agreed. "And now that you are going to allow Jonathan to go with us next time, you could ask him to help watch for her, too."

Mandie glanced at the clock on the bureau. "Celia, I think I have time to go down to the lobby and look around for Molly before everyone assembles for supper," she said, standing up quickly. "I'll be right back." She jumped up and opened the bedroom door. No one was in the sitting room they shared with her grandmother.

"Oh, Mandie, please hurry. Your grandmother may not like it if you're gone when she's ready," Celia called after her softly.

Mandie put her finger to her lips for her friend to be quiet. Then she opened the door to the hall and hurried to the lobby of the hotel. There were lots of guests milling around, but no poor little Irish girl. Mandie went outside and walked around the courtyard but still saw no sign of the child.

"Oh, well," she sighed disappointedly, heading back inside, through the lobby and halls and toward her room.

"No sign of her," Mandie told Celia as she barely made it to the settee before her grandmother opened her bedroom door and joined them. Soon after, Jonathan and Senator Morton entered the room.

"Why don't we eat here in the hotel tonight," Senator

Morton suggested. "I hear there's a concert scheduled later in one of the rooms downstairs."

"Downstairs?" Mandie questioned. "We *are* downstairs, aren't we?"

"Yes, but there is another floor below us," the senator explained. "It's mostly for entertaining and such."

"I agree. Let's do that," Mrs. Taft said. "We can always take our walk after the concert."

When Senator Morton inquired about the hour of the concert, they found supper would have to be hurried in order to make the schedule.

Mandie had left Snowball in their room and would have to take him something to eat.

"You'll just have to take the time to run some food to Snowball and then get back to the concert room as fast as you can. We'll save a seat for you," Mrs. Taft told Mandie.

"Yes, Grandmother," Mandie said as everyone finished the meal and stood up. She took a saucer and piled it full of leftovers.

"Come on, Amanda, we'll show you where the stairs are so you can find the way," Mrs. Taft told her.

Senator Morton led them into the hall and then to a far corner where the staircase was located.

"All right, I can find the way," Mandie told them. "I'll be right back." The others descended the stairs to the concert room while Mandie hurried to her room with Snowball's supper.

Once inside, she placed the saucer in the bathroom and gave the kitten fresh water in a bowl supplied by the hotel. "I have to shut you up in here until we get back, Snowball," she told him. "But we're going for a walk later, and I'll ask Grandmother if I can come back and get you."

She closed the door and hurried out of the suite and

down the hallway. Suddenly she heard a hissing sound and someone calling her name. She stopped to look around and was surprised to see Molly crawl out from behind a huge settee in the alcove at the end of the corridor. The little girl came toward her.

"Kin ye go huntin' leprechauns now?" Molly asked.

"Oh, Molly, where have you been? We looked for you at number nine Murphy Lane," Mandie told her.

"I been lookin' for a leprechaun," Molly said.

"But, Molly, do you really live at number nine Murphy Lane?" Mandie asked.

"Sure'n I do," Molly said. "That be my home place."

"But, Molly," Mandie said. "Celia and I went into that house and there's not even any furniture in it. All the rooms are filled with junk."

"Oh, but miss, number nine Murphy Lane do be my living place," Molly insisted. "Me mither and me, we live under the ground there."

Mandie was shocked. "Under the ground? What do you mean?"

" 'Tis under the ground we live," Molly insisted. "There be two rooms there. We have two beds and furniture. Not junk like upstairs."

Mandie finally understood. "Oh, you mean you live in the basement?"

The child nodded. "And we don't be usin' the front door of the place. We be havin' our own door and steps in the back. The main floor, it be empty. Nobody lives in it."

Mandie sighed with relief. At least it was the right address. But what kind of a home was it in the basement, Mandie wondered.

"Molly, my grandmother is waiting for me and I can't stay to talk, but I'll try to catch up with you later tonight,"

Mandie told her. "We're going to a concert downstairs right now. When it's over we're going for a walk. Maybe I'll see you then."

"I'll be waitin' in front of this hotel," Molly said.

Mandie waved to her and hurried to the steps to join her grandmother and the others. Molly *would* show up now, when she couldn't get away. And of all things, living in the basement of that house. Mandie hadn't noticed that it had a basement. She would investigate for herself, with Jonathan's help, of course. Never would she visit that neighborhood alone again.

Chapter 6 / What's Molly Up To?

Mandie enjoyed the concert, which was presented by the local Irish Society. Variations of classical and Irish ballads were played, and the music was lilting and lively. The young people glanced at one another now and then and smiled. Evidently Celia and Jonathan liked the presentation, too.

In fact, the concert was so enjoyable to Mandie that it seemed to come to an end too soon. She could have sat there another hour or two. Then, suddenly, she remembered Molly. As they left the room with the crowd, Mandie whispered to her friends.

"I met up with Molly in the hallway when I came back from feeding Snowball, and she said she would wait outside for us," Mandie said under her breath.

"Did she say anything about looking for leprechauns?" Jonathan asked as they entered the hallway.

"Yes, but I didn't know what to tell her about that. I don't know when we'll have a chance to go with her,"

Snyder County Library
Selinsgrove, PA 17870

Mandie explained. "But she told me she does live at nine Murphy Lane—in the basement."

"I don't remember seeing a basement," Celia remarked.

"It's probably completely underground without any windows," Jonathan said. "At least that explains something."

"Let's go back there and see exactly where she lives," Mandie suggested as they moved with the crowd.

"What for?" Jonathan asked.

"I'd like to know what kind of a home she has," Mandie explained.

"Amanda, come along, all of you," Mrs. Taft said as she and Senator Morton ascended the stairs.

Mandie remembered Snowball. "Grandmother, I need to run and fetch Snowball so he can have some fresh air, too."

"Well, make it fast," her grandmother said. "We'll wait for you in the lobby."

"I'll hurry," Mandie promised. "Celia, you and Jonathan watch for Molly, will you?"

"Sure," the two agreed as they followed the adults, and Mandie rushed back to her room.

Snowball had licked his saucer clean, and was curled up on the big bed. When his mistress opened the door he stood up, stretched, and began washing his face. Mandie grabbed his red leash from the bureau and reached for him.

"Sorry, Snowball, we don't have time for you to freshen up right now," she said as she fastened the leash and picked him up. "I'm going to carry you to the lobby. It's faster that way." She cuddled him in her arms and rubbed her cheek on his soft, furry head. He began to purr with contentment.

Mandie found everyone waiting for her in the lobby. Jonathan and Celia shook their heads to indicate they had not seen Molly. Mrs. Taft and Senator Morton led the way outside, and Mandie and her friends looked all around the front of the hotel, but Molly was nowhere in sight. It was dark now, but gas lights illuminated the street.

"Let's walk this way," Mrs. Taft suggested as she and the senator turned left up the street.

The three young people followed, keeping a lookout for the little Irish girl. They were passing a bakery when Mandie finally spotted her. She was sweeping the floor with a broom that was much taller than she was.

Mandie called to her as she and her friends stopped in front of the shop. "Molly!"

The little girl immediately dropped the broom and came running. Mrs. Taft and Senator Morton strolled ahead without noticing.

"Now ye kin hunt for leprechauns?" Molly asked with a big smile as she rubbed her dirty hands on the same dress she had been wearing before.

"Not right now, Molly. Why were you sweeping the floor in there?" Mandie asked.

"I sweep, then Miz Blaine gives me sweet rolls," the child explained.

"Well, you didn't finish your job. You'd better go back and do that so Mrs. Blaine will give you the rolls," Mandie told her. "We have to walk with my grandmother awhile, but we'll be back soon. We'll look for you then, all right?"

Molly frowned, and looked up at Mandie. "Be ye tellin' me the truth? Ye will be back?" She stooped to rub Snowball's fur.

"I promise, Molly," Mandie told her. "We won't walk very far because my grandmother is probably tired by now. We'll have to return this way to get back to our hotel.

Now you go finish your sweeping and enjoy the sweet rolls."

Molly stood up and sighed. "That I will, but it's huntin' leprechauns I'd rather be."

The young people started to walk on as Mrs. Taft glanced back to check on them. Mandie threw Molly a kiss as the little girl slowly walked back into the bakery.

"Are you planning on coming back outside after we return to the hotel and your grandmother and the senator go to their rooms?" Jonathan asked, keeping pace with Mandie as she hurried to catch up with Mrs. Taft and Senator Morton.

"If possible," Mandie said.

"You aren't planning to go back to Molly's house tonight, are you? It's dark now," Celia said anxiously.

"I don't know for sure," Mandie replied. She was thinking it would be awfully dark at night on Murphy Lane because she didn't remember seeing a single street light. She wondered if Molly's mother would be home. What hours did she work anyway? Molly seemed to run freely at all hours.

When the three young people reached the adults, Mrs. Taft told them, "We've just spotted an outdoor cafe ahead, and we thought maybe you'd all like something sweet to eat, or something to drink."

The three brightened immediately. "Yes, ma'am," they chorused.

Mrs. Taft smiled and said, "Well, come on then, and don't fall so far behind again."

The little cafe had approximately a dozen chairs surrounding small white tables. A huge green awning extended from the front of the building over the dining area. Small green candles in glass holders lit up the tables.

"Such a pretty place," Mrs. Taft remarked as the senator pulled out a chair for her. The young people quickly sat down, too. They were elbow to elbow at the tiny table.

A robust woman with dark hair and a big smile came to wait on them. She wore a green and white checked dress with a big white apron over it. " 'Tis a nice night for walkin'," she said to Mrs. Taft.

Mrs. Taft smiled at her and said, "Yes, it is, but we need something to get us back."

"Irish puddin', that be the best liked," the woman said.

Mrs. Taft looked around the table and said, "I believe I'll just have tea, please. Anyone want pudding?"

The three young people immediately ordered the Irish pudding, and Senator Morton took hot tea.

"Maybe this will pep me up for the walk back," Mrs. Taft said with a smile at Senator Morton. "I didn't realize we had come so far."

"We might be able to catch a hack," Senator Morton suggested as he looked out into the street.

"No, no, that won't be necessary. We just won't walk as fast going back," Mrs. Taft replied as she sipped her tea. "This is delicious."

"So is the pudding, Grandmother," Mandie said around a mouthful. She had taken the saucer from under the dessert dish, put a spoonful of the pudding on it, and placed it under her chair for Snowball, who was eating it noisily.

"What would you all like to do?" Mrs. Taft asked unexpectedly. "We probably have two days left here in Belfast."

The young people looked at one another, and Mandie asked, "Just two more days?"

"Yes, we have to wait for Uncle Ned, you know," her grandmother explained, "and we don't know exactly when he is coming. He said he would be here at least by the end of this week, which is two days away."

"Then Uncle Ned could be here sooner?" Mandie questioned.

"Yes, dear. Now, what shall we do with the rest of our time here?" Mrs. Taft asked again.

The three young people had the same answer. "The play!" they said almost in unison.

"Yes, the play about the leprechauns," Mandie added. "Please, Grandmother?"

Mrs. Taft looked at Senator Morton and asked, "Did you find out where the theater is located?"

"It's not far if we hire a carriage. Maybe fifteen or twenty minutes away. It's across town," Senator Morton explained.

The three young faces broke into smiles as Mrs. Taft said, "All right then. We'll see the play. But we'll have to find out the hours. Now, what else?"

Mandie knew her friends were thinking the same thing she was. They didn't want to get tied down to a busy schedule and have no time left to hunt for leprechauns.

When no one answered, Mrs. Taft said, "Well, think about it and let me know. I believe we'd better start back now. It's bedtime if we're going to be up early in the morning."

As they passed the bakery on the way back to the hotel, the young people lagged behind. Pausing to look inside, they saw no sign of Molly.

"Do you think she got tired of waiting and went home?" Mandie asked her friends.

"I could ask the woman in the bakery," Jonathan volunteered.

Mandie grabbed his arm. "No, Jonathan, don't do that."

"Maybe she's around the hotel," Celia suggested.

They walked on until they reached the entrance of the hotel. While Senator Morton held the door for Mrs. Taft, the three quickly fanned out across the courtyard searching for Molly, but she was nowhere to be found.

"Amanda, what are y'all doing? Come along now," Mrs. Taft called to them when she looked back and saw them scurrying around.

"Yes, ma'am," Mandie answered, almost out of breath. Celia and Jonathan joined her, and they entered the hotel.

Their eyes searched the lobby as soon as they were inside, but Molly was not in there either. As they came into the wide hallway Mandie glanced toward the huge settee in the alcove where the little girl had been hiding before. Molly emerged cautiously from behind the piece of furniture, and stood there looking at the young people.

Mandie noticed that her grandmother and the senator were a good distance down the hallway. She whispered to the child, "Wait right here. I have to go to my room with my grandmother, but I'll be right back. And my two friends will, too."

Molly sighed, placed her dirty hands on her hips and said, "Ye be all the time tellin' me to wait. I wait, wait, wait. I be tired of waitin'. I be needin' to look for the leprechauns."

"I'm sorry, Molly, but I will be right back, really. Please trust me just one more time, all right?" Mandie said.

"This be the last time I wait then," Molly said with a frown. "Ye be fast or I be gone."

"I will," Mandie promised.

Molly crawled back behind the settee where she could watch the three young people hurry down the hall after the adults.

Once the good-nights were said, Mandie and Celia

went into their room. Mandie took off Snowball's leash and sat down.

"We'll have to wait a few minutes to be sure Grandmother doesn't come looking for us," Mandie told Celia.

"Do you think we really ought to do this, Mandie?" Celia asked. "Maybe we ought to ask your grandmother if we can go back outside."

"Oh, no," Mandie quickly replied. "I don't know whether she would agree to it or not, but we don't need to bother her about it. We aren't doing anything wrong. We're just going back to see Molly."

"She may be gone by the time we get back to the lobby," Celia said. "She seems to move around pretty fast."

"Come on. Jonathan ought to be in the hallway by now," Mandie told her. The girls quietly opened their bedroom door, then closed it behind them to keep Snowball inside. As Mandie opened the door to the corridor, she found Jonathan leaning against the wall waiting for them.

"Let's go," Mandie whispered to her friends.

They quietly made their way back to the lobby and to the alcove where Molly said she would wait. Mandie expected the little girl to be watching and come out from behind the settee, but as they approached it there was no sign of her. Mandie ran to the settee and looked behind it. Molly was not there.

"She didn't wait!" Mandie exclaimed in a disappointed voice.

"Maybe she's outside," Jonathan suggested.

"Maybe," Mandie said as the three went out the front door.

They looked around the courtyard, and suddenly Molly appeared behind Mandie, causing her to jump.

"Here I be," Molly said as Mandie whirled around.

"Oh, Molly, you're as elusive as a leprechaun yourself," Mandie said with a smile.

"What be 'lusive?" Molly asked.

"You are always appearing and disappearing," Mandie explained. "Now let's walk down to your house, and you can show us where you live."

Molly looked at her and said, "There be no leprechauns in my house." The three young people laughed.

"I know," Mandie said with a smile. "But I'd like to see where you live so I'll know where to find you if I want to see you again."

"But I niver stay in the house, 'cept when me mither is not workin', and lately she be workin' all the time, seems to me," Molly said with a frown.

"Well, anyway, we'd like to see your house," Jonathan told her.

Molly backed away and stared at Jonathan. She looked at Mandie and asked, "Ye be allowin' him to hunt leprechauns? Ye said—"

"I know," Mandie interrupted. "But I've decided we need him. You see, he's big and strong and he can help hold the leprechaun if we catch one." *Or anyone who may try to attack us*, Mandie added silently.

"Ye don't plan on givin' him part of the pot o' gold, do ye?" Molly asked.

Mandie looked at Jonathan. He was grinning. "He doesn't need the pot of gold. And Celia and I don't, either. We don't want any of it. If we found a pot of gold we'd give it all to you," Mandie assured her.

"So be it then. We be on our way," Molly said, walking toward the street.

The young people followed Molly along Murphy Lane until they came to the old house where they had been earlier. Molly turned and walked around the house. Once they were behind the dwelling, Mandie saw the steps going down to the basement.

The little girl began descending the stairs, and the three followed. It was pitch dark and they had to feel their way.

"Molly, don't go so fast. We can't see," Mandie told her as she stayed right behind the child.

"Be light soon enough," Molly told her. As they reached the bottom of the steps Mandie saw a faint light ahead.

Molly led them down a narrow passageway into a room that was dimly lit by an oil lamp.

"Here we be," Molly said with a sigh of relief. "Now, kin we look for leprechauns?"

Mandie and her friends looked around. There was a fireplace at one end of the room with ashes in it. A decrepit settee stood at the other end, and in between there was a small table and two straight-backed chairs.

"Where is your bedroom?" Mandie asked.

Molly immediately pushed back a curtain that was hanging near the fireplace and led them into a room with two beds in it. Clothes were hanging on a wire extended from wall to wall. The beds were made up, but Mandie decided Molly must have done it because the covers were not exactly straight.

"Don't you have any windows?" Mandie asked, looking around the top of the walls.

"Don't need windows. Only let the cold in," Molly said.

"Where do you keep your food?" Celia asked, not seeing a kitchen.

"Keep our food?" Molly looked at Celia, puzzled. "We don't keep food. We eat it."

The three young people looked at one another in dismay. Evidently Molly and her mother were too poor to have any food around except what they ate. And Mandie wondered how much food they really consumed.

"Did you eat today?" Mandie blurted.

"That I did," Molly said with a smile, rubbing her tummy. " 'Tis good food I ate today. The cook at ye hotel give me food for pickin' up garbage in her kitchen."

"When will your mother be home, Molly?" Mandie asked.

"That I don't be rightly knowin'," the child said. "But now we be lookin' for leprechauns?"

"Let's go," Mandie told her friends.

Molly led the way back outside, and once they were in front of the house she stopped and said, "Now, I be thinkin' there may be leprechauns down this way." She pointed down the street where it intersected with another.

"Shall we follow her?" Mandie asked her friends.

"Why not?" Jonathan said.

"Let's not go into any more old houses," Celia said.

Molly was enjoying the search. She kept darting ahead, causing the others to run in order to catch up with her. She suggested going down one street, and then quickly switched to another street. She led them through backyards of houses where people were living. Now and then someone would wave to her. All the time she was laughing and calling back to her friends, "This way. No, that way. I think I saw one go down that lane!"

Finally Mandie was tired of the game, and she rushed ahead to put her hand on the little girl's shoulder to stop her.

"Molly, I think we'd better go back to the hotel now. My grandmother might miss us," Mandie told her.

The little girl looked up at her and said, "Ah, but we be just beginnin'."

Mandie smiled at her as Celia and Jonathan stood

patiently nearby. "But, Molly, it's dark, and we're all tired. Let's see if we can do this again tomorrow. If you'll watch for me at the hotel tomorrow morning, I'll let you know what time we can continue our search."

Molly shrugged and said, "So be it. Sun come up in the mornin', I wait for ye." She turned and ran ahead until they entered Murphy Lane again.

When they reached the house where Molly lived, she simply waved to them and disappeared around the back.

"Well, that was interesting," Jonathan said with his mischievous grin.

"It sure was," Mandie agreed.

"I think she just wants us to play with her," Celia said. "She probably doesn't have any friends, and her mother must work nearly all the time."

"Do y'all want to go on a search for leprechauns again tomorrow at whatever time we have free?" Mandie asked as they walked toward the hotel.

"The daytime would be better. That way we can see where we're going," Celia remarked.

"You can count me in," Jonathan said.

Mandie stopped, as she had a sudden thought. "Maybe Uncle Ned will get here tomorrow, and we can get him to go with us."

Jonathan laughed and said, "I'm not sure Uncle Ned would agree to go looking for leprechauns."

"We'll find that out when he gets here," Mandie said as they went to their rooms for the night.

Chapter 7 / To Catch a Leprechaun

The next day was sunshiny and warm again. The girls were the last ones to arrive at the breakfast table. Senator Morton said he had been up at dawn and had already gone for a walk.

After everyone was seated at the table and the food had been ordered, Mrs. Taft told the young people, "Senator Morton has the schedule for the play that you all wanted to see. There is a performance this morning. He and I think it would be better to go to a morning showing and have the rest of the day free for other things."

"Oh, thank you, Grandmother!" Mandie said excitedly as the waiter brought the coffee, and a waitress served the food.

"I appreciate the chance to see it, too, Mrs. Taft," Celia spoke up as the uniformed attendant poured coffee into the cups.

"So do I," Jonathan said with a big smile. "In fact, I appreciate the opportunity of traveling with all of you, and

I thank you." He began eating the meal.

"Well, Jonathan, you are most certainly welcome. It has been nice to have you accompany us. Oh, by the way, I believe Senator Morton received a wire from your father this morning," Mrs. Taft said, turning to the senator.

The senator cleared his throat and looked at the boy. "I was going to wait until after breakfast to tell you about that, because I'm afraid you're going to be disappointed," he said. "You see, the wire stated that your father would be unable to catch up with us here in Ireland—"

"I knew it! I just knew it," Jonathan interrupted. "He's never going to catch up with us at all." He sighed dejectedly.

Mandie reached over and patted Jonathan's hand in an attempt to console him. "That's all right, Jonathan. You'll get together with him soon, I'm sure, but in the meantime just think of all the exciting adventures you are having with Celia and me."

Jonathan quickly pulled his hand away and tried to smile as he replied, "You're right. There'll never be a journey like this again. I'd better enjoy it while I can."

"I'm afraid you didn't allow me to finish what I was saying, Jonathan," Senator Morton said.

"I apologize, sir. I'm sorry I interrupted you," Jonathan said.

"There was more to the message. I am to keep your father posted as to where we're going next, and he will try to wind up the business transaction he's currently negotiating, and meet us at our next stop," Senator Morton explained.

"Thank you, sir, but isn't this journey through Europe for you people about to end? You only have Scotland and Wales left to visit. Then it's London and home, right?" Jonathan picked up his fork again and pushed the potatoes around on his plate.

"I imagine your aunt and uncle will be back home in Paris by then. The newspaper they work for said they would return shortly when I checked with them by wire last week, remember?" With a twinkle in his blue eyes Senator Morton added, "That's where you really want to go, and I think your father will allow that."

"I've been thinking about my aunt and uncle," Jonathan replied. "You see, they're only in Paris for a certain length of time. They have a contract with the newspaper as foreign correspondents, and when that expires they may just decide to return home to New York."

"Well, if they do, maybe you can visit them there for a while," Mrs. Taft said. "That is, if your father is not going to be at home."

"He's never at home. That's why he's always sent me to boarding schools all over the world," Jonathan said with a sigh.

"Then perhaps you will attend a school somewhere here in Europe, and Amanda could enter one near yours," Mrs. Taft suggested.

Mandie quickly drew in her breath. *Why is she bringing this up again?* she thought. Celia quickly placed her hand on Mandie's arm, causing Mandie to reconsider the remark she was about to make. *I will not go to school in Europe, not ever,* she said to herself.

Jonathan merely raised his eyebrows and resumed eating.

When the meal was finished, Senator Morton pulled out his pocket watch, at the end of a long chain, and said, "Perhaps I'd better go out and engage a carriage while you girls freshen up."

"That's a good idea," Mrs. Taft said. "Amanda, take something to Snowball and hurry back. I'll wait in the lobby. Celia, Jonathan, if you go to your rooms for anything, please make it fast."

Mandie quickly put some scraps of food on a saucer for her cat.

"I'll just wait with you in the lobby, Mrs. Taft," Jonathan said as the senator left the room.

Celia went with Mandie to their room. Snowball was sitting right behind the door when Mandie pushed it open. He stood up on his hind legs and begged for the food she was carrying.

"Oh, you poor little thing. You act like you're starving to death," Mandie told him as she went into the bathroom. "Come on, in here."

Snowball followed her and immediately began gulping down the food, now and then making deep purring sounds of contentment.

Celia stood before the mirror, tucking loose tendrils of her auburn hair under her bonnet. "What do you think your grandmother will want to do this afternoon, Mandie?" Celia asked.

Mandie came to stand beside Celia and said, "I have no idea. She hasn't said a word about it. You know, I wish Uncle Ned would hurry up and get here. I want him to meet Molly. I think they will find each other interesting; he with his Cherokee accent and she with her Irish brogue." She giggled. "They may not understand a word the other one is saying."

"You're right. Sometimes it's hard for me to understand Molly. I'm used to Uncle Ned's accent though," Celia replied.

"You know, Grandmother can't understand Uncle Ned sometimes. That's because she doesn't have a drop of Cherokee blood in her. But I suppose because my father's mother was Cherokee, it never has been hard for me to figure out Uncle Ned's speech." Turning abruptly from the mirror, Mandie said, "Let's go."

"Yes. We don't want to be late for the play," Celia agreed.

They found Mrs. Taft and Jonathan in the lobby, and as they entered, Senator Morton came in through the front door of the hotel.

"I have a carriage waiting," the senator told them. "I've engaged the man for this morning, and told him we'd probably want a carriage this afternoon as well."

The young people looked at one another.

"Yes, that's a good idea I suppose, even though we haven't fully decided where we'll be going this afternoon," Mrs. Taft said as the senator held the door to the hotel open for her.

"Psstt!" Mandie heard from the shrubbery in the courtyard. She looked around and spotted Molly squatted down nearby and beckoning to her.

When Mandie saw that her grandmother and the senator were about to board the waiting carriage, she quickly darted across the grass and told Molly, "I'm sorry, but I have to go with my grandmother this morning. Maybe we'll be around later this afternoon."

"That bein' the case, I'll jist hafta go huntin' all by meself then," Molly said, a disappointed look on her face.

"We're going to see a play about leprechauns," Celia said cheerfully as Mandie and Molly approached the sidewalk.

"Ye be goin' to *see* leprechauns?" Molly asked, her blue eyes wide.

"Not real ones. Just some people who pretend they are. We'll tell you about it when we see you again," Mandie told the child as she and Celia hurried toward the hired vehicle.

Molly stood watching as they drove off, and Mandie waved to her through the open window.

"She is lonely, isn't she?" Jonathan remarked.

"Yes. I wish there was something I could do for her. She doesn't have a grandmother like I do, or even a mother who can spend time with her," Mandie said. "I never know when I'll see her, and she probably doesn't believe me when I say I'll see her again, or that I'll hunt leprechauns with her when I get the chance."

"I think she understands you have to do whatever your grandmother plans for the day," Jonathan said.

"If only Uncle Ned would come. Maybe then Grandmother and Senator Morton would find something to do alone and leave us with Uncle Ned," Mandie said.

They drove through the downtown area of Belfast and on out to the edge of the city before they came to the theater. There was already a line of carriages discharging their passengers at the front door, but before long it was their turn.

The young people quickly examined the posters at the front of the theater. A copy of the one they had seen at the hotel hung near the door, and several others on either side showed various actors made up as leprechauns.

"This is going to be fun," Mandie said as they followed the adults inside.

Mrs. Taft held on to the senator's arm in the darkness as a uniformed attendant took their tickets and showed them to their seats. The rows were staggered in a descending fashion toward the stage, and when Mandie sat down she was glad to see she would have a clear view of the performance.

A thick, green velvet curtain covered the stage, and Irish music could be heard from behind it. Posters with large green shamrocks painted on them hung at each end of the platform.

The theater was filled in just a few minutes, and a tall man in a green suit came through the center closing of the curtains and walked downstage. The music was lowered to almost a whisper.

"Ladies and gentlemen," the man began. "Welcome. We hope you will be comfortable and will enjoy our play as we portray the early history of Ireland. We ask that you do not attempt to catch one of our leprechauns, though, because they do not have a pot of gold."

The audience laughed loudly.

A man called out, "But the title of your play is *Catch a Leprechaun.*"

Everyone laughed again.

"So it is. But you'll have to find one someplace else, if you really are after gold," the man answered, laughing to himself. "We couldn't produce this play without our leprechauns. I'll be quiet now and let you see for yourself. Thank you."

The man stepped back through the opening in the curtain, to the wild clapping of the enthusiastic audience. The music went back up, and the heavy green curtain began slowly parting.

Mandie watched eagerly as leprechauns sitting on little stools began hammering on small shoes. Then she remembered that the word leprechaun was Gaelic for shoemaker.

"I say," the leprechaun on center stage began speaking, "would that our ancestors had beaten down the Fomorian invaders. Then we would not be at such tasks."

"Ah, but remember, Balor of the Evil Eye led the Battle of Moytura," the leprechaun on the left said as he paused in his work.

"Aye, and we had no one who could fight the evil magician because of his third eye, which blasted fire over our people," the leprechaun on the right said.

The leprechaun in the center spoke again, "Me da, and his da 'fore him, and his da 'fore him, and on to those at the beginnin' of time have repeated the story. They said this was what happened."

The lights dimmed, and the curtain closed. The young people squirmed in their seats, anxious to see what would come next.

In a few seconds, the music changed to a loud march tune as the curtain reopened. Warriors in ancient attire faced each other, brandishing slugs and sticks, as one group came from the left and one from the right. A huge man with wild-looking hair and three big eyes on his face led the group from the left.

A loud whisper rose from the warriors on the right. "Ah, Balor of the Evil Eye." They shrank together as they watched the huge man slowly approach them.

Suddenly Balor of the Evil Eye turned his third eye on the defending warriors. What looked like fire, but what Mandie knew must be light from a lantern hidden under the mask, suddenly beamed on the man's prey. The men began dropping one by one until they were all lying on the floor of the stage.

Balor of the Evil Eye turned off his third eye and paraded downstage and proclaimed, "Hereafter the Tuatha De Danann race will be banished underground forevermore."

The music came up again and the curtain closed.

The audience seemed to be enjoying the play. They clapped vigorously and called out things that Mandie couldn't understand above the noise. She turned to her friends and said, "I wish Molly could see this."

Jonathan laughed and said, "Oh, no. She probably would have run right up on stage and chased the leprechauns."

As the music quieted, the curtain reopened. Huge rock-like mounds, surrounded by green grass, covered the stage. There was a grunting noise, and finally the rock in the center cracked and a leprechaun emerged. He blinked his eyes, shook his head, and stomped his feet. Gradually the other rock formations burst open, and soon the stage was full of leprechauns.

They were all dressed alike, in old-fashioned green frock coats with seven large silver buttons, knee-length trousers, and long white stockings. The toes of their shoes turned up, and they were adorned with large silver buckles. Three-cornered hats sat atop their wiry red hair. Leather aprons covered the fronts of their short pants.

Mandie was close enough to see that their noses were hooked, and when they grinned their mouths expanded from ear to ear. They were each about three feet tall, maybe a little more, and Mandie wondered if the actors were children or dwarfs. She knew they wore heavy makeup in order to look alike.

A leprechaun in the center spoke. "And so, Balor of the Evil Eye made leprechauns of us. Now we emerge into the world again."

"And we go about our shoemaking trade," another one said from the left.

Each leprechaun found a grassy spot, sat down cross-legged, and began pulling things from his apron pocket; a half-made shoe, a tiny hammer, and tacks, which he secured in the corner of his mouth.

As they began tapping away on their shoes, they also began talking.

"At least, as leprechauns, we know we'll be inhabiting this earth for nigh onto three hundred years, so let that be a warning to save for ye livelihood," one said.

"Aye, I already have me pot of gold, well hidden,"

another said with a big wink.

"These earth people will do ye out of it, if ye give 'em half a chance," another one said.

"That'd be right hard to do," the first one said. "Recall that man who snatched me by the tail of my frock coat and threatened to squeeze me life out if I didn't lead him to me pot of gold? I outdone him, that I did. When I told him to look yonder at the bushes by the creek, where the pot of gold be, he got too excited and I slipped away."

"Shouldn'ta let him catch ye in the first place," one said. "Ye must disappear, like me. None of 'em ketched me yet."

Mandie and her friends were totally immersed in the play, as the cast went on to portray leprechauns being chased by people who wanted their pots of gold. It seemed that no one had ever been able to hold on to one of the creatures, that is, if they were lucky enough to catch one.

When the performance was over, the young people excitedly discussed the play. Mandie was more determined than ever to help Molly look for a leprechaun. She was more convinced they might be real beings, and she wanted a chance to find out.

As they left the theater, Senator Morton suggested getting something to eat in the neighborhood because it boasted several fine cafes that served the theater patrons.

"I'd like to get out of the crowd and relax for a few minutes," Mrs. Taft explained to the senator. "How about that indoor one on the corner?"

"That looks good to me. Let's try it," the senator agreed. Because they had managed to get a head start on the crowd leaving the theater, they got to the restaurant ahead of the others and were able to sit in a private alcove and be served almost immediately.

The young people talked excitedly about the play while the adults carried on their own conversation.

"Oh, they looked so real!" Mandie exclaimed.

"They *were* real," Jonathan said with his mischievous grin.

"Oh, Jonathan, you know what I mean. They weren't really *leprechauns*. They must have been either children or dwarfs made up to look like the little green men," Mandie said.

"I wonder how I would look in all that get-up," Jonathan said, smiling at Mandie.

"Please don't ever try it. You'd never make a good leprechaun," Mandie said with a laugh. "For one thing, you're too tall."

"Evidently all leprechauns are men," Celia remarked.

"Come to think of it, you're right," Mandie said.

"Then the race will never multiply. That must be why they live to be three hundred years old," Jonathan observed.

"Oh, but didn't you hear one of them say they live in little homes underground? They probably have wives down there," Mandie said with a big smile. "Somebody has to stay home and cook."

Mrs. Taft noticed the young people were doing more talking than eating. "Amanda, y'all eat up now. We don't want to spend the rest of the day in this cafe."

"Yes, ma'am," she said, lifting a forkful of potatoes to her mouth.

"If only Molly could have seen the play," Mandie whispered between mouthfuls. "I'd sure like to have seen her reaction."

"I'm sure she would have thought it was all real," Jonathan said, breaking a roll and buttering it.

"Mandie, do you know where we're going next?" Celia asked in a low voice.

"No, but I do hope we have a chance to catch Molly again in the daylight. That way we can see where we're going," Mandie said.

As soon as everyone was finished eating, Mrs. Taft gathered her things and rose from the table. The young people overheard her say to the senator, "I believe I'd just like to get back to the hotel and rest for a while. I'm beginning to think I am too old for all this gadding about all day long."

Mandie tried to suppress a huge smile.

"Come now, you're just a young lady," the senator said to Mrs. Taft with a twinkle in his eye. "Much younger than I am."

"Oh, Senator," Mrs. Taft said.

Mandie was surprised to see her grandmother actually blush. She turned away to smile at her friends.

Senator Morton and Mrs. Taft led the way outside, and Jonathan whispered to the girls, "Love knows no age."

Mandie stopped short, her mouth wide open. "Do you think my grandmother is in love with the senator?" she asked.

"Well, it certainly looks like it to me," Jonathan muttered under his breath.

"What would be wrong with that, Mandie?" Celia said in a low voice.

Mrs. Taft turned to speak to them before Mandie could answer Celia. "Senator Morton will walk to the corner and get our carriage. We'll go back to the hotel and rest awhile. I think all of you should write your parents too. I haven't seen you mail any letters lately. This afternoon would be a good time to do it."

"Grandmother, I write to my mother often," Mandie

said. "You wouldn't know it, because I haven't mailed most of them. I thought I'd take them all home as a diary of my thoughts for my mother."

"What a good idea, Amanda," Mrs. Taft said as they stood waiting. "However, Elizabeth needs to hear from you now and then."

"Yes, ma'am," Mandie said. "I'll write her a letter and mail it this afternoon. I promise."

"And I'll write my mother, too," Celia said.

"Since my father is traveling around the world, I wouldn't know where to send a letter to him," Jonathan said sadly.

"Write the letter anyway," Mrs. Taft told him. "If you don't find out where to mail it, you can give it to him when he finally catches up with us."

Senator Morton returned with the driver and the carriage, and they all got in to drive back to the hotel.

Mandie and her friends kept an eye out for Molly as they neared the hotel grounds, and they even looked behind the huge settee in the alcove when they arrived inside, but the child was nowhere around.

Senator Morton stopped at the front desk, and the rest of them continued toward their rooms. Then the senator hurried to catch up with them, calling to Mandie.

"Your Uncle Ned has arrived," the senator told her, smiling. "He has a room next to Jonathan's. The man at the desk said he thought he would be in his room now."

"Oh, Grandmother, Uncle Ned is here!" Mandie exclaimed. "Couldn't Celia and Jonathan and I spend the afternoon with him instead of writing letters? We could write the letters tonight before we go to bed."

Mrs. Taft smiled thoughtfully. "Oh, all right, dear. But please promise me that you will all write letters sometime this evening."

The three nodded in the affirmative.

Mandie practically ran down the hall. Jonathan and Celia hurried after her. Uncle Ned was here and things would get more interesting.

Chapter 8 / Uncle Ned Helps Hunt

As Mandie raced down the corridor, she almost collided with Uncle Ned, who was just leaving his room. The old Cherokee smiled and bent to embrace her.

"Papoose, what big hurry?" he asked as Mandie returned his hug.

"Oh, Uncle Ned, I heard you were here, and I'm just so glad you've finally arrived!" Mandie told him.

"So am I, sir," Jonathan said, extending his hand.

"I am, too, Uncle Ned. We need you," Celia said.

The old Indian looked questioningly at Celia, and then at Mandie.

Mandie put her hand on the sleeve of his deerskin jacket. "We really do need you, Uncle Ned. We've met a little Irish girl, and she wants us to help her look for leprechauns. Do you believe in them? Is there such a thing?"

The old man chuckled to himself. "Papoose, you find mystery everywhere you go. I walk now. Need fresh air." He started down the corridor with Mandie on one side and Jonathan and Celia following on the other.

"Let's go and sit on the wall outside," Mandie said. "There's a little park out near the front entrance."

"Yes," Uncle Ned agreed. "Talk better when sit."

When they neared the huge settee where Molly had hidden before, Mandie ran ahead to see if the child might be waiting there. But Mandie was disappointed again. *Why isn't she around now that Uncle Ned is here to help us?* she thought to herself.

Outside, sitting on the wide, low wall in the park, Mandie excitedly related their adventures in Ireland. "You didn't say if you believe in leprechauns, Uncle Ned," she finally asked. "Do you?"

The old Indian frowned slightly and repeated the word slowly, "Le-pre-chauns? What Papoose know about them?"

"They are little men who wear green clothing. They have red hair, and each owns a pot of gold. The Irish people believe in them," Mandie tried to explain. "We saw a play this morning that showed the history of these people."

"Gold?" The Cherokee seemed far away in his thoughts. "Papoose remember cave back home? Find gold there."

"Oh, yes, Uncle Ned, I remember," Mandie said. She knew he was referring to the Cherokee legend in the Nantahala Mountains. "But the Irish believe these little men have a pot of gold stored away somewhere, and if you can catch a leprechaun you can make him lead you to his pot of gold."

"Papoose speak of fairies," he said with certainty. "Irish fairies."

"You're right, Uncle Ned," Jonathan said. "But some people claim these little men are fairies who do good."

"The word leprechaun means shoemaker in Gaelic," Mandie added. "I want you to help us catch one, Uncle Ned." She looked up at him eagerly.

Uncle Ned looked at each of the young people. "All believe in fairies?"

"Maybe," Mandie said.

Jonathan shrugged his shoulders, and Celia just smiled.

"The little Irish girl we met is named Molly," Mandie began, "and she definitely believes in leprechauns. She has hunted for them, and even seen them, but they always get away before she can catch one. She and her mother are poor. Molly would like to find a leprechaun's pot of gold so her mother won't have to work so hard. Anyway, she asked us to help her."

Mandie stopped to watch Uncle Ned's reaction. The old Indian had joined them on many adventures, but she wasn't sure he would agree to go chasing "fairies," as he called them.

"Papoose, not possible to catch fairies," Uncle Ned said seriously. "Fairies not real. Can't put hand on them."

"But, maybe leprechauns are different—a different kind of fairy," Mandie suggested hopefully. She noticed Jonathan's smile, but continued, "Would you agree to come along with us—just for the fun of it? Please, Uncle Ned." She looked pleadingly at her old friend.

Uncle Ned thought for a moment, then smiled and said, "I go to watch Papoose and friends. Where Irish papoose live?"

"Oh, thank you, Uncle Ned! I knew you'd agree," Mandie said, jumping down from the wall and reaching for his wrinkled hand. "Come on, we'll show you where Molly lives."

Mandie led the way to Murphy Lane, and the others followed.

"Bad place to live," Uncle Ned said, shaking his head.

"Yes," Mandie agreed. As they neared Molly's house, she told him about the man who had grabbed her when she and Celia had entered the house alone. "We said we would never come here again alone. But we feel safe with you, Uncle Ned."

"Papoose be careful. Think before act," the old man cautioned, his face showing concern.

"I know, Uncle Ned." Mandie stopped in front of number nine. "This is the house."

"Fall-down house. Not good," he muttered to himself. "Irish papoose live here?"

"In the back," Jonathan volunteered.

"It's in the basement, and there aren't any windows down there," Mandie explained.

When they descended the stairs, they found the door open and a lamp burning inside. "Molly, are you home?" Mandie called.

"No one home," Uncle Ned observed, looking around.

"Well, I guess we can search the neighborhood for her," Mandie offered. She turned to lead the way back upstairs.

As they reached the yard, Uncle Ned asked, "Who live with Irish papoose?"

"Just her mother," Mandie affirmed. "And she works all the time in the linen mill, so Molly runs free, looking for leprechauns."

"Poor people," Uncle Ned remarked. "Like some Cherokee people."

"Yes, Uncle Ned. That's why Molly wants to catch a

leprechaun, so she can find his pot of gold."

Uncle Ned frowned. "Not possible, Papoose."

"Which way shall we go?" Jonathan asked as they stood on the street in front of the house.

"That way," Mandie pointed to the cross street ahead.

"Let's not get lost, Mandie," Celia said worriedly.

"We won't," Jonathan assured her. "We've been all over this neighborhood before."

As they walked along, they kept watching for Molly. Finally they found themselves in front of what looked like an overgrown park.

"I don't remember seeing this place before," Mandie remarked.

"We didn't come here with Molly, I'm sure," Celia said. "Oh, I hope we aren't lost."

"We're not lost," Jonathan said. "It's a straight line from here to the back of Molly's house."

Mandie looked at Uncle Ned. "Do you think we could explore this park? Maybe Molly is hiding in here."

"Stay together," he answered. "Watch for sharp limbs, holes in ground."

The three nodded, and Jonathan led the way, with Celia right behind him and Mandie and Uncle Ned bringing up the rear.

They had not gone far when Jonathan suddenly stumbled.

Mandie gasped when she saw what he had stumbled on. A man's leg, clothed in torn, dirty pants, was protruding from the bushes.

The old Indian quickly bent to touch the leg. "Leg not dead," he announced.

The three young people hung back as Uncle Ned stooped to see who the leg belonged to. As he stuck his head through the thick brush, there was a loud, terrifying scream, "Glory be!"

The leg instantly retreated, and a dirty, ill-kempt figure crawled out from under the bushes and away from Uncle Ned. Mandie knew the man was frightened, but most people were when they first encountered the Indian. His deerskin jacket, leggings, and clattering shell necklace were not normal apparel, especially in Ireland.

"He won't hurt you," Mandie quickly told the man.

When Mandie spoke, the man's eyes grew big. "Ye be the one that visited number nine!" He scrambled to his feet and ran into the dense bushes and out of sight.

Then Mandie realized he was the man who had grabbed her in the dark room. "That's the man I told you about, Uncle Ned," Mandie said.

"She's right," Jonathan acknowledged.

"Gone now. Smell bad. Whiskey. Ugh!" Uncle Ned wrinkled his nose.

Mandie nodded. "He was probably drunk again."

"Shall we go on?" Jonathan asked.

Celia sighed as Mandie quickly agreed, and she and Uncle Ned walked on ahead. Jonathan and Celia followed closely. The old Indian snapped off small twigs here and there to mark their trail, and Mandie knew they wouldn't get lost.

Eventually they stepped through a thicket and found themselves in a grassy clearing with a little stream running through it. Wild flowers seemed to bloom everywhere they looked.

"It's just like a picture book!" Mandie exclaimed in delight.

"I wouldn't know. I'm too old for picture books," Jonathan said cleverly.

Mandie stopped and put her hands on her hips. "Very

funny, Jonathan. I'm sure you had your share of picture books when you were small."

"I hear something!" Celia said in a loud whisper, wrapping her arms tightly around herself.

Uncle Ned seemed to know instinctively what it was. "Animal. Stay here." He started forward to investigate a clump of bushes ahead of them.

Mandie, Jonathan, and Celia watched silently.

As he neared the bushes something shot out from under them. Mandie gasped in surprise. "It's a cat!" The gray kitten stopped short at Mandie's legs, but when she stooped to touch it, the kitten batted its paw at her with claws extended.

"Strange cat, Papoose. Do not touch," Uncle Ned warned.

"But, Uncle Ned, he seems to be awfully tame," Mandie said, bending to talk to the cat.

"Papoose!" Uncle Ned's voice was stern.

"All right, Uncle Ned. It's good I left Snowball in our hotel room. They would probably get into a fight," Mandie said.

"Let's go in another direction," Jonathan said.

"All right," Mandie said as she led the others to the left, where a trail curved out of sight.

Uncle Ned continued breaking twigs along the way, and Mandie looked down to see the kitten following them. She smiled to herself. No one else seemed to notice the animal.

The trail led through a wooded area with small stone houses here and there between the trees. Though they were old, the homes looked well-kept. Most of them had flower gardens about the doorways.

"This is like a picture book, too!" Mandie said excitedly. "It's picture perfect."

"I think so, too," Celia said. "Wouldn't this make a beautiful painting?"

"Maybe the leprechauns live here," Jonathan teased.

Uncle Ned smiled slightly at the boy.

"Oh, Jonathan, I wish one would come out of that house over there," Mandie said, pointing. "You'd probably run away if you saw one."

At that very moment, the door to the house Mandie had indicated opened. A small figure stepped outside. Mandie blinked her blue eyes in disbelief and ran toward the house. "Molly! What are you doing here?"

Molly had apparently not seen them and was walking away from the house, her back to the others. When she heard Mandie's voice, she stopped and turned around. "Ah, ye be here! Ye lookin' for leprechauns?" When she saw Uncle Ned she stopped in fright. "Who be that?"

Mandie smiled and put an arm around the girl. "He's one of my dearest friends. I call him Uncle Ned. He's a real Cherokee Indian."

Molly shook her head slightly. "I never heard o' Indians. Who he be kin to?"

Everyone smiled at the little girl. Mandie looked at Uncle Ned. He was smiling, too.

"He came from the United States. He is my father's friend back home," Mandie tried to explain.

Molly looked at Mandie curiously. "But ye said your father was not in this world."

"He isn't. But when he was alive, Uncle Ned was his friend." Mandie took the girl's hand. "Don't be afraid. He won't hurt you." The child nervously held back.

"Uncle Ned, this is Molly, the little Irish girl we told you about," Mandie said.

Uncle Ned squatted to Molly's level and said, "Irish papoose. Love." He smiled as his shell necklace rattled.

Molly's eyes were riveted on the shell necklace around Uncle Ned's neck. "Love? Ye love me?" she asked.

"Yes, Papoose Molly. Love everybody," the old man replied.

Suddenly the gray cat appeared out of nowhere and began rubbing itself against Molly's legs. She gasped when she saw it. "Ye brung me a cat?" she asked Mandie.

"Well, not exactly," Mandie began. "We found it in the bushes back there, and it followed us. I think he likes you."

"I like it," Molly said, stooping to cuddle the animal. "Now we look for leprechauns?"

"First tell me what you were doing in that house over there," Mandie said.

"That house?" Molly asked. "I work there. I sweep the missus' floors and she gives me soup."

"I'm glad," Mandie said. "You sweep the bakery and Mrs. Baines gives you sweet rolls, and you sweep this woman's house and she gives you soup. I guess you won't go hungry, will you?"

"I say not," Molly said, shaking her head. "I gets all me wants, one way or t'other. Now we look for leprechauns?" She looked up at Uncle Ned. "Will he come with us?" she asked Mandie.

"Of course," Mandie said. "He's big and strong, and good at tracking through the woods. He won't let anything happen to us. Which way should we go?"

Molly looked around. "That missus, where I sweep floors, says leprechauns can be found that way." She pointed straight ahead down the trail.

Mandie looked at Uncle Ned. He smiled and nodded at her. "We walk awhile. Then we go back to hotel. Soon time for supper."

"Let's not go too far," Celia said. "We might get lost."

"No," Molly assured her. "Me knows the way."

"All right. Let's get going," Jonathan said.

"Don't run off and leave us, Molly," Mandie cautioned.

"I be sure ye be followin'," Molly said, holding tightly to the gray kitten.

"You see what I mean, Uncle Ned?" Mandie said softly. "She really believes there are leprechauns."

Uncle Ned shrugged. "Maybe we find one."

Mandie looked up at her friend and smiled. "Who knows? Maybe we will."

Chapter 9 / All Over Belfast

Molly led Mandie and her friends into a part of Belfast that they had not seen before. It appeared to be the wealthy section. Enormous stone houses with fancy carriages in the driveways lined the wide boulevards. Now and then a motor car sputtered by. Ladies in the latest fashions, mostly escorted by handsomely dressed men, paraded down the avenues.

Jonathan remarked, "This street could almost be mistaken for a street in New York."

"Well, I've never been to New York," Mandie said as the group came to a halt at an intersection. "But I do know I've never seen such wealth, not even in Washington."

"What about Paris, Mandie?" Celia asked.

"Paris looked older. It didn't look fresh and new like this city," Mandie answered. "The French people were more informal, too, not all dressed up like these people."

Molly jumped up and down as she squeezed the kitten

in her arms. "Me thinks the leprechaun went that way!" She pointed to a side street leading off the boulevard on the opposite side.

"This, last street. Must go back to hotel," Uncle Ned said as the group followed Molly across the boulevard.

Mandie slowed down on the side street to stare at the shops, which were filled with rich-looking merchandise. The stores were colorfully painted and sported awnings over the doorways. They passed a jewelry store, a dress shop, a hat shop, a men's shop, a book shop, a candy shop and many more.

The sidewalks were narrower here, and Mandie noticed that when they passed a well-dressed person, the person would usually look back and seemed to single out Molly. Mandie didn't think it surprising, considering the faded, dirty dress Molly wore and her uncombed hair. Mandie wished again with all her heart that she could do something for the little girl. Maybe her grandmother would agree to buy some new clothes for her.

Suddenly Molly broke away from the group and raced across the street. "The leprechaun went in there!" she said, darting into a candy shop.

Mandie and her friends quickly followed. As they reached the doorway, the proprietor was demanding that Molly leave his shop.

The tall, gray-haired man had a long beard and was waving his hands at Molly. "Out with ye! Out. Out," he was saying.

Molly stood on tiptoe at the counter and snatched a bonbon from a crystal bowl. Then she turned and fled.

Mandie stood with her mouth open.

The man, not knowing Molly was with them, smiled at Mandie and asked, "What might I do for you, miss?"

Before Mandie could answer, the man spotted Uncle

Ned. He waved his hands at the old Indian, shouting, "Out! Out! You are not wanted in here."

Mandie couldn't believe her ears. The man seemed anxious to get rid of Uncle Ned. But the old Indian just stood there silently.

Mandie spoke to the proprietor. "What are you doing? Uncle Ned is with us. So was that little girl who just ran out."

The man straightened his shoulders and said, "I can pick and choose my customers. I don't need the likes of them." He turned back to Uncle Ned and said, "I asked you to leave."

Uncle Ned continued to stand still, his arms folded across his chest.

Mandie, furious with the attitude of the man, whirled around and announced, "We will all leave." As she turned, her skirt caught a large crystal bowl sitting on a low table. The bowl fell to the floor, breaking into pieces and scattering its contents of candy all over the floor.

The man yelled angrily at her, "Ye won't leave till ye pay for this!"

"I don't owe you a penny. It was an accident. And you were rude to us," she called back as she flounced out of the shop.

Jonathan and Celia, at a loss for words, followed Mandie outside, and Uncle Ned came after them.

Mandie couldn't see Molly anywhere. "I think we've lost her again," she said. "Oh, well, it's time we went back to the hotel anyway. I'm hungry. Can you find the way back, Uncle Ned?"

"This way," Uncle Ned replied, walking quickly down the street.

Jonathan glanced back at the candy shop they'd just left. "It's a wonder that man didn't call for the police, Mandie," Jonathan told her.

Mandie slowed down. "What for? I should have called for the police when he tried to throw Uncle Ned out of his store."

The old Indian, hearing her comment, reached to pat Mandie's shoulder. "No, no, Papoose. I not leave until ready. No one make me leave. Must forget. Forgive."

Mandie grasped her old friend's wrinkled hand. She felt the hurt Uncle Ned must have experienced with the shop owner's attitude toward him.

"I was shocked when Molly stole that bonbon," Mandie said. "She must have known she was wrong, because she ran off and disappeared."

"Papoose Molly need love, teaching," Uncle Ned said.

"She should be spanked for snatching that candy," Jonathan added.

"My mother would have spanked me for such a thing when I was her age," Celia said.

"Must teach first," Uncle Ned said as they crossed the wide boulevard. "Then not learn. Then spank."

When they started down another side street, Mandie realized that Uncle Ned was not taking them back the way they had come. "Uncle Ned, we are not going back by the same streets."

"Papoose Molly not come in straight line. We go straight way. Shorter, faster," the old man explained.

"I sure wish I had as good a sense of direction as you have, sir," Jonathan told him.

"Practice," Uncle Ned said with a smile. "I live long time. Practice, always."

"I'd like to visit you in North Carolina and practice following trails with you," Jonathan said, looking up at the old man.

"Yes. Come. Stay my house. Soon," Uncle Ned invited him.

"Oh, yes, you'll have to stay at Uncle Ned's house and meet his wife, Morning Star. She makes the most delicious owl stew I ever ate," Mandie said, grinning at Jonathan. "And he also has a beautiful granddaughter, Sallie, who lives with him. She's about my age."

"Now I know I'm going for a visit!" Jonathan said.

"And you must visit Mandie, too, because there is another pretty girl who lives next door to her," Celia added. "Her name is Polly."

"She might be pretty, but she's a scaredy-cat," Mandie said with a frown. "She's afraid of her own shadow."

Jonathan grinned and looked at Celia. "Any more pretty girls near your house?"

"No, but lots of beautiful horses," Celia said. "We raise thoroughbreds."

"How exciting," Jonathan said. "Seriously, I wish you would all come and visit me in New York. That is, if I get to stay home and go to school there this year. I'd love to show you our city." He looked up at Uncle Ned. "And you, too, sir. You'd be most welcome at our house."

Uncle Ned smiled. "Some day," he said.

"You would go to New York?" Mandie asked excitedly. "Then I'd go with you, Uncle Ned."

"Must ask mother first," Uncle Ned said.

"Oh, I will, of course. And, Celia, you could go with us, too," Mandie said to her friend.

"That would be a lot of fun," Celia replied.

Before long, Mandie spotted their hotel ahead. "We're almost back. There's the Shamrock Inn," she said.

As they walked through the small park at the front of the building, Mandie looked around, half expecting to see Molly jump out of the bushes or something. *Chasing leprechauns! What a joke!* she thought. Then she remembered the play. "Uncle Ned, the hotel lobby has a poster advertising that play I told you about. Come on. I'll show you," Mandie said as they entered the lobby.

Mandie hurried to the counter where they had seen the advertisement. The poster was still there, but the man was not behind the desk.

"The actors in the play looked just like leprechauns, too," Celia said.

"We couldn't decide whether they were dwarfs or children," Jonathan added.

Uncle Ned stepped closer and inspected the poster. "These are fairies we chase?" he asked.

"These are actors from the play," Mandie said. "But according to Molly, there are real leprechauns floating around somewhere."

Uncle Ned shook his head as he looked at the poster, but he didn't say anything. Mandie wondered if he thought differently of leprechauns now that he knew what they looked like.

"We go now," Uncle Ned said abruptly. "Be late for supper."

Mandie sighed. "We'd better not be late, or Grandmother won't like it. She probably wonders what we did all afternoon."

"And I'm starving," Jonathan moaned. "See you girls later." He and Uncle Ned went on down the hallway to their rooms.

The girls entered their sitting room. Snowball was curled up asleep in the middle of the big bed when Mandie and Celia opened their bedroom door. Mrs. Taft's bedroom door was closed.

"If we hurry, we should be ready by the time Grandmother is," Mandie told Celia.

The girls rushed about, washing up, and pulling out fresh clothes. They were ready and waiting in the sitting room when Mrs. Taft opened her bedroom door to join them.

"I'm glad to see you girls are on time," Mrs. Taft told them.

Just then, Uncle Ned and Senator Morton entered the small room, and Jonathan followed close behind. He took a seat between the girls on the settee.

"Have you decided where we will eat tonight?" Senator Morton asked, after Mrs. Taft had greeted Uncle Ned. She had not seen him since his arrival at the hotel that afternoon.

"Why don't we eat in the dining room of the hotel. That will save time, if we are going out to the river afterwards," she replied.

"Fine. I was going to suggest that," the tall, handsome senator said. Turning to Uncle Ned he asked, "Is that all right with you, sir?"

"Good," Uncle Ned said. "I travel lots today. Rest tonight."

"Oh, Uncle Ned, do you mean you aren't going with us to the river?" Mrs. Taft asked.

"Rest. Travel all last night. Sleepy," the old Indian told her.

Mandie, listening to their conversation, complained, "But, Uncle Ned, you always go with us everywhere when you're around. Remember you promised my father you would watch over me." She smiled up at him mischievously.

"Grandmother, senator watch over Papoose tonight. I watch tomorrow,"Uncle Ned said. "Must sleep."

"Tomorrow then," Mandie conceded.

Mrs. Taft rose and said to Mandie, "Amanda, you might as well bring that cat and tie him under the table so you can feed him there. That way we'll be ready to go as soon as we finish eating."

"What are we going to do at the river, Grandmother?"

"We are going on a moonlit boat ride. The river is way beyond the linen mill, so it will take us a while. Let's all go down to the dining room and eat."

Mandie whispered to her friends when they entered the corridor after the adults, "I wonder if there could be any leprechauns on the river."

"Maybe," Jonathan said, "but I thought you'd given up on them."

"I doubt it, Mandie," Celia said.

"I wonder where Molly is. She's really avoiding us, I think, since she took that candy," Mandie said as they entered the dining room.

"We may never see her again," Jonathan said, pulling out chairs at the table for the girls.

"I'd like to see her one more time just to give her some clothes, or something," Mandie said with a sad expression. "I really feel sorry for her."

"So do I, Mandie," Celia agreed. "But there's not much we can do for someone like her, who doesn't even live in our country where we can see her often."

"Besides, there must be thousands of poor people in the world, and we can't help all of them. We wouldn't have enough time, or money," Jonathan reminded the girls.

"Well, let's all keep a watch out for her when we leave the hotel," Mandie said. "She may be around somewhere."

After they had dined, and Snowball had been fed from a saucer under the table, the group prepared to leave for the river. The three young people walked more slowly, and looked in every nook and cranny on their way out, and then in the courtyard outside, but there was no sign of Molly.

Senator Morton had already arranged for a carriage to take them to the river. The driver had the vehicle waiting out front. The adults stepped inside ahead of the young people, when suddenly Snowball, walking at the end of his leash, managed to pull away from Mandie and race off into the bushes. Mandie and her friends went after him.

"Amanda, please get that cat and hold on to him," Mrs. Taft called to her from the window of the carriage.

Snowball darted for the rear of the hotel. Mandie called to her friends, "Y'all go that way and I'll go this way so we can block him off."

Jonathan and Celia hurried to the left of the hotel and Mandie ran to the right. Mandie was just in time to see Snowball streak through a partly opened cellar door. She lunged after him, but he was too fast for her.

Wall sconces lit the area, and Mandie found stairs going down. Snowball must have taken this route. There was nowhere else he could have gone. She stepped down one step cautiously, and then another, in an effort to see inside the cellar. Snowball had disappeared.

"Just one more step," Mandie murmured to herself, peering into the dimly lit stairwell. Then she took another step, another, and another, until she reached a landing. She called to Snowball, hoping he would come back up so she wouldn't have to go any farther.

She could see rows of shelves containing jars and sacks of food going all the way into the dark recesses of the cellar. Moving slowly downward, she called to Snowball again.

Suddenly, out of the corner of her eye, Mandie caught a movement behind a row of shelves. The shadow was too large to be Snowball. She caught her breath and froze, staring ahead. She heard a faint noise, and scanned the cellar as her eyes adjusted to the darkness. Just then a small figure of a man, about three feet high, dressed all in green, darted behind a row of jars. The silver buttons on his jacket and the buckles on his shoes glinted in the dim light. *A leprechaun!* Mandie exclaimed to herself. *I don't believe it! I don't believe it!*

The little man stared back at her and then seemed to evaporate among the shelves. Mandie finally mustered the strength to turn and run back up the stairs. Snowball almost tripped her as he came flying out of the cellar and up the steps ahead of her with his fur puffed up in fright.

When Mandie reached the outside door, she stepped into the yard and leaned against the wall of the hotel to catch her breath. Snowball had stopped at her feet, just as Jonathan and Celia rounded the corner.

"Where were you Mandie? What's wrong?" Jonathan asked, hurrying to her side. "You're as white as a ghost." He picked up Snowball and held him tightly.

"I—I—" Mandie began, unable to finish.

Celia grasped Mandie's hand and rubbed it. "Mandie, do you feel faint? Should we get your grandmother?"

Her remark released Mandie from fright. "No, no, I'm all right, but—" she hesitated, looking at her friends. "Y'all are never going to believe this—"

"Oh, come on, Mandie. We've got to get back to the carriage," Jonathan urged.

"All right, then, to make it to the point. I chased Snowball into the cellar, and I saw a real, live leprechaun down there," Mandie quickly said as she watched her friends' expressions turn into surprise.

"I don't believe it. You must have imagined it," Jonathan said.

"A real, live leprechaun, Mandie?" Celia asked, her eyes growing big.

"Yes, a real live leprechaun. I don't care whether you believe me or not, Jonathan Guyer. I know what I saw." Mandie snatched Snowball from him and ran around to the front of the hotel, and to the carriage.

Jonathan and Celia stepped inside the carriage behind Mandie and took their seats. They all remained quiet on the ride to the river.

Mandie knew Jonathan thought she was making something up. Celia, forever the peacemaker, did not say anything to add to the problem.

Mandie was so upset by having seen the creature in the cellar that she couldn't even remember what her grandmother had said when the three finally got into the carriage. She made sure she held tightly to her cat's leash as he sat in her lap.

I'll talk to Uncle Ned about this, as soon as I get a chance, Mandie said to herself. He was always the first one up in the morning. She'd be dressed and waiting for him to come down the hallway at daybreak.

Suddenly, the carriage came to a halt and the driver appeared at the door. "Sorry, madam, but I smell smoke and see light in the sky. There must be a fire somewhere ahead. Do you wish to continue?" he asked.

Everyone immediately stuck their heads out the windows to see what the man was talking about. Senator Morton opened the door and stepped outside.

"Oh, dear," Mrs. Taft exclaimed. "What should we do?"

"A fire!" Mandie said, holding more tightly to Snowball.

Senator Morton appeared back at the doorway to the carriage. "I can't tell whether the fire is on this road or not. I suggest we go on a little farther and find out," he told Mrs. Taft.

"All right, Senator," Mrs. Taft agreed. "Please tell the driver we'll go on until we tell him to stop."

With that done, they continued down the road. Everyone kept watching to see where the fire was. Suddenly, they were jolted to a halt as the horses reared up and refused to go on.

The driver came to the passenger door again. "The horses smell smoke and will not go any farther, madam. I can tell now where the fire is. 'Tis the old linen mill, that's for sure."

"Are we near the mill?" Mrs. Taft asked.

"It's around the next bend in the road, madam," the driver said.

"Well, I suppose we'll have to turn around and go back to the hotel," Mrs. Taft said. "It's a shame the old mill is burning. Can you tell whether it's bad or not?"

"Not from here, madam, but I can walk ahead and find out for you," the driver said.

"Yes. Let me take a look, too," Senator Morton said as he stepped down from the carriage.

"May we go too, Grandmother, please?" Mandie begged.

"I suppose we could all walk ahead instead of sitting here not knowing what's going on," Mrs. Taft reasoned.

The senator helped Mrs. Taft alight from the carriage, and the three young people followed excitedly. They all walked down the road, which was illuminated faintly by the light of the fire.

Chapter 10 / Fire!!!

When they came within sight of the mill, Mandie had trouble holding on to Snowball, who was obviously frightened by the fire. He squirmed and clawed, but he didn't manage to escape his mistress.

The fire seemed to be confined to one section of the structure. Mandie could see flames coming out one window, and smoke filled the air. She glanced at her dress and could see tiny black specks floating down onto it. She wondered if her grandmother had noticed. They had all stopped on the road to look.

"What happened?" Senator Morton asked a man standing nearby.

"Don't know yit, but 'tis bad, that I can see," the man replied.

Firemen had pulled the horse-drawn fire wagon up as close to the building as they could and were dispensing water from it. Dozens of people stood watching.

Mandie edged closer to a group standing nearest to

them in an effort to overhear their conversation. They were discussing the fire, but because of their Irish brogue, Mandie couldn't understand what they were saying. Jonathan and Celia joined Mandie, while Mrs. Taft stood on the road holding on to the senator's arm. Mandie looked back to see her grandmother dab at her nose with a handkerchief, and now and then fan her eyes as the smoke became thicker.

A young man in the group that Mandie and her friends were listening to spoke more clearly. "Too bad. Must be something someone can do. Can't just let her die in there."

Mandie sprang forward, touched the young man on his sleeve, and asked, "Is there someone inside the mill?"

"Aye, 'tis a little child—" He stopped as a woman came rushing through the crowd and headed straight into the burning building. He caught his breath. "That's the child's mother."

The firemen tried to stop the woman, but she managed to crawl through an open window and disappear inside.

Goose pimples ran all over Mandie as she quickly moved toward the firemen. Celia and Jonathan followed close behind her.

"Can't you get those people out of there? A man back there says a little child is inside, and now her mother has gone in, too," Mandie asked one of the firemen who was struggling with the water hose.

"No, lass, part of the inside wall has fallen. We know where the little girl is, but she's trapped behind the timbers and we haven't been able to break through yet. There are firemen inside the building," the man said.

Mandie felt her heart beating faster and faster as she looked frantically about. She felt so helpless. Some little girl was about to be burned alive. Couldn't anyone save her?

She turned back to the fireman who was still struggling with the water hose, and begged, "Can't you get enough men inside to move the timbers? Do something! We can't just let her die in there!"

Suddenly, Mandie heard a voice screaming inside the old mill. "Molly! Molly! Where are you?"

Mandie knew at once that it was the little Molly they knew. It had to be. Her mother worked in the mill. But she asked the man, "Is that the Molly whose mother works in the mill, and who lives at nine Murphy Lane?"

The man paused to look at Mandie and said sadly, "I be afraid 'tis her. Ye know her?" He went on about his work.

"Oh, yes, we know her. Please, mister, where is she inside? Is she in the section that is on fire?" Mandie had tears in her blue eyes, and her voice quavered.

Celia and Jonathan had overheard everything, and Celia was dabbing her eyes with her lace handkerchief. Jonathan kicked at the dirt with the toe of his shoe.

"No, miss," the man said. "But she be surrounded by the fire and must come through it to get out."

Mandie turned to her friends and handed Snowball to Celia. "I'm going in after her," she declared.

Celia missed her grasp on the cat, and Snowball managed to get away. He disappeared into the shrubbery nearby, but Mandie didn't even notice.

The fireman overheard Mandie's remark and said, "No, miss, we can't allow that. The hole is not big enough for our men to crawl through, and you might not make it either without the timbers being moved. The men inside are trying to clear a path now."

"I'm going after her. I'm smaller, and I can probably

crawl through," Mandie said determinedly.

"If you are going in, then I'm going, too," Jonathan said.

"Maybe I can help, too," Celia said nervously.

Again, the young people heard the screams inside, and ignoring the pleas of the firemen, the three ran around the building and out of sight. They searched for a window that the fire had not reached. Suddenly, Mandie pulled her friends to a halt and held their hands. "Our verse," she said. "Let's repeat it together."

And they did. " 'What time I am afraid I will put my trust in Thee.' "

Mandie added, "Please God, save Molly and her mother."

Without another word, Mandie led the way through the open window and dropped into the smoke-filled room. It was hard to see through it, and the three felt their way to the far wall before finding the firemen working in the next room attempting to move the huge timbers that had fallen. The wood was crisscrossed every which way, blocking the entrance to the next room.

Suddenly, the screams of the woman looking for Molly were heard again, and the young people located her in a room to their right. She was trying to move heavy timbers herself, when all at once they gave way and knocked her down, trapping her beneath.

Mandie screamed, and the firemen hurried to help the woman, who was silent. The three young people were holding their handkerchiefs to their noses, and Mandie yelled through hers, "It's up to us now. Let's go."

They entered the first room again, where the firemen had been working, and Mandie squatted down to look through the pile of wood. There was an opening not far off the floor. "I think I can get through here if y'all will hold on to the wood and make sure it doesn't cave in on me," Mandie told Jonathan and Celia.

"If it starts to cave in, I don't think we'll be able to stop it," Jonathan warned her.

Mandie paused, and then said boldly, "I'm going to take a chance. Just stay here and watch for me to come back through." She threw off her bonnet, pulled her long skirts tightly around her, and started wriggling through the opening in the woodpile.

"Please, God, let me make it. Let me get Molly out, please, dear Lord," she said softly as she tried to move forward. She took a deep breath with her handkerchief over her nose and then called out, "Molly! Molly! It's me, Mandie. Where are you? Can you hear me?" And then Mandie almost lost her breath in the smoke. She started coughing, but she kept wriggling forward. The splintered timbers tore her clothes and scratched her face and hands, but she didn't even feel it.

"Here I be," came a weak voice from the other side of the woodpile.

Mandie's eyes filled with tears of joy as she recognized Molly's voice. "Don't move. I'm coming after you," Mandie called to her again. And suddenly she was through and found the little girl crouching in a corner of the room with her dress pulled up over her head.

"Molly!" Mandie cried as she ran forward. "Don't talk, just crawl through that space under the woodpile, and I'll be right behind you."

"Mandie, there's fire out there!" Molly cried as Mandie put her arm around her. "I'm asceered o' fire, that I be."

"Come on, Molly, you can't stay here. The fire will be in here in a few minutes and you won't be able to get out at all," Mandie coaxed her. She pulled the child to her feet and pushed her toward the opening she had come through. The smoke was so dense she had to feel to find the place again. She forced the child into the small passageway in the wood, and Mandie went in right behind her.

"We're—coming—out!" Mandie tried to call to her friends, but her voice was weakened by the smoke.

Jonathan and Celia were waiting to pull Molly through as she appeared. Then they reached a helping hand to Mandie. Just then, Mandie felt her long skirt catch on the wood, and there was not enough room for her to reach down and pull it free. She wriggled and tugged while her friends stood bravely by.

"Get the fireman. I'm stuck!" she managed to say.

"You're only about two feet from the opening," Jonathan told her. He knelt down to try to see inside. "Can you reach my hands?" Mandie tried, but she was too far away.

Molly shoved Jonathan aside and said, "I kin get back in there." The child stooped down and scrambled part way in. "Give me yer hand," she called to Mandie.

Mandie reached forward and grasped Molly's hands. They held tightly to each other. Molly tried to pull and back out at the same time but was not strong enough.

Jonathan stooped down again. "Mandie, hold tight to Molly and I'll pull on Molly's dress."

He pulled hard, but the dress didn't tear. Molly and Mandie came out of the small opening so fast Jonathan was knocked backward. He scrambled to his feet and said, "We've got to get out of here. The fire is spreading!"

"Where are the firemen?" Mandie asked. By now, she was dripping with sweat and covered with soot.

"They're still trying to get the woman in the next room out from under the timbers," Jonathan said. Grabbing Mandie's hand on one side, and Molly's on the other, he rushed toward the open window through which they had entered the building. He picked up Molly and shoved her through first, then helped the other girls through before following them onto the ground outside. They rolled in the grass trying to get their breath, and then managed to take Molly to a safe distance from the burning mill.

Jonathan and Celia spoke to the firemen in the yard, telling them Molly had been rescued.

Mandie knelt down to examine the little girl. "Are you all right?" she asked, ignoring her own scrapes and bruises.

"Me throat is sore," Molly said, coughing loudly.

Mandie suddenly saw the strange woman from the ship talking to her grandmother as they stood across the yard. And of all things, the woman was holding Snowball in her arms. She couldn't hear what they were saying, but the woman hurried toward Mandie with Mrs. Taft right behind her. Mandie looked down at her ruined clothes and knew her grandmother was going to be awfully put out with her.

The strange woman reached Mandie first. She quickly handed Snowball to Mandie and quickly disappeared into the crowd before Mandie could say a word. Senator Morton rushed to join her grandmother.

Mrs. Taft took one look at Mandie and Molly before saying in a shaky voice, "Amanda, you could have been killed! What ever made you do such a thing? When I found out y'all were inside that building I nearly had a heart attack!"

"I'm sorry, Grandmother," Mandie said, holding tightly to Snowball. "But Molly was trapped inside, and the firemen were too big to get through the timber to rescue her. Her mother is trapped in there—" As soon as she said the words, Mandie realized the child had not been aware that it was her mother inside. Before anyone could stop her, Molly began running across the yard, screaming loudly, "Mummy! Mummy!"

Jonathan and Celia, returning from speaking to the firemen, saw Molly running toward the building. Jonathan was able to stop her and bring her back, kicking and screaming, to Mandie.

Mandie handed Snowball to Celia and put her arms around the child, saying, "Molly, the firemen are in there with your mother. There is nothing you can do to help."

Molly relaxed in Mandie's arms. "They'll get her out, won't they?" she asked, her voice trembling.

"Don't worry. Those firemen are trained to rescue people. They know what to do," Mandie told her.

Mrs. Taft asked, "Amanda, who is this child?"

"Her name is Molly. We met her on the street the first day we were here, and we've seen her now and then since," Mandie explained. "Her mother works in the mill there."

Molly wiped her tears as she said sadly, "And I've been tryin' to find a leprechaun and git his pot o' gold so me mither won't have to work so hard." She looked up at Mrs. Taft.

"Where is your father, child?" Mrs. Taft asked.

"Me father is not in this world, he's not," Molly told her. "He left before I can remember."

"Why did you go into that mill? Was it burning when you went inside?" she asked.

"No. I seen a leprechaun go in there, I did," Molly said. "And I followed him to see if his pot o' gold be there. But I couldn't find him after he turned over the lamp that set the mill on fire."

"Someone turned over a lamp and set the mill on fire?" Mandie asked in surprise. "Jonathan, go tell the firemen. Someone else may still be in there besides Molly's mother."

At that moment, Mandie saw the firemen carrying Molly's mother out of the building on a stretcher. They took her toward a waiting fire wagon.

Mandie held on to Molly, knowing the child would try to get to her mother. Mandie hurried toward the wagon in an effort to get a glimpse of the woman on the stretcher, all the while holding tightly to Molly's hand. When they were close enough, Mandie could see that the woman was either dead or unconscious.

"Me mither!" Molly cried, trying to break loose from Mandie's grasp.

"No, Molly, your mother has been hurt and the firemen will take her to the doctor. We'll see her later," Mandie told the child.

After speaking to the other firemen about the fact that someone else might be in the building, Jonathan had asked about Molly's mother.

Turning to the girls, he said, "They are taking your mother to the hospital for a few days, Molly."

Tears streamed down Molly's soot-covered face. "To the hospital? Can I go, too? I can't go home by meself," she sobbed.

Mandie turned to her grandmother, who had walked over to where they stood. "Molly lives alone, Grandmother, with her mother." Mandie's voice was shaking. "And it's a terrible place. We've been there with Uncle Ned."

"All right, Amanda, I know what you're saying. We'll take her back to the hotel with us, just for the night, mind you, and you will have to give her a bath," Mrs. Taft said.

"She needs clean clothes, too, Grandmother," Mandie said. Molly held tightly to her hand.

"Very well, I'll ask the driver where we can find a shop to get something for her. Now let's be on our way," Mrs. Taft said. "We'll be leaving Ireland tomorrow, or as soon as a boat sails, to return to London and pick up our things from the hotel there. We're going home right away."

Mandie and her friends stood there listening in surprise. "Grandmother, I'm sorry if I've spoiled your trip—" Mandie began.

Mrs. Taft cut her off. "We won't discuss it right now."

"I'll get the driver to bring the carriage as close as possible," Senator Morton was saying. "The firemen seem to have put out the blaze."

The others walked slowly to the road as Senator Morton went on ahead. When the driver finally pulled the carriage up in front of them, they all gladly climbed into it.

On the trip back to the hotel, Mrs. Taft and Senator Morton carried on a low conversation of their own, and Mandie couldn't understand what they were saying.

She turned to her friends as they discussed the fire in soft voices. Molly, overcome with weariness, fell asleep at last on Mandie's shoulder.

"What about her—?" Mandie mouthed the word "mother."

Jonathan whispered back, "The firemen told me she may not make it, but if she does, will most likely be permanently disabled."

"Oh, no!" Mandie whispered. Her blue eyes filled with tears, and she wiped them with the back of her hand. As soon as she did it, she realized she must have blackened her face with more soot and grime.

Celia whispered, "What will become of her?" She pointed to Molly, and Mandie's eyes grew wide. She hadn't thought about that. If her mother was permanently disabled how would they live. They barely existed now.

Jonathan said quietly, "Orphanage, probably."

Mandie shook her head vigorously. "No, no, no! I've heard those places are awful! I couldn't let her go there."

"But what will you do?" Celia asked softly.

Mandie thought for a moment. "Maybe there are relatives," she said.

After they got into the heart of town, the driver pulled the carriage to a stop and came back to speak to Mrs. Taft. "There is a shop across the street, madam, where you will find children's clothes," he said.

"Thank you. We won't be long," Mrs. Taft said. Then looking at the young people, she added, "Since none of you is fit to be seen in public, I shall have to attend to this myself. Senator Morton, would you accompany me, please?"

"Certainly," the senator said. He left the carriage and assisted her out.

Mrs. Taft turned again to the young people. "No one is to leave this carriage while we are gone. Do you understand?"

"Yes, ma'am," the three chorused.

The young people watched as the adults crossed the street and entered a clothing shop. The driver waited outside the carriage.

"Well, I suppose I've ruined things for everybody," Mandie told her friends. She looked down at Molly, whose head was now in Mandie's lap. "But Molly might not have gotten out in time if I hadn't gone in after her." She pushed back a strand of hair from the sleeping child's face.

"Don't blame yourself, Mandie," Jonathan said. "I went in with you."

"I take as much blame as you do," Celia said.

"It seems so uncharacteristic of Grandmother to suddenly decide to go home because of what we did. Usually she gives me a good talking to and then forgets about it. But not this time," Mandie said sadly, wondering about Mrs. Taft's sudden decision to return home.

"Well, one good thing about it, we only had Scotland and Wales left to see," Celia said. "At least we finished most of our journey."

"Yes, and I really am looking forward to seeing my mother and my baby brother, and Uncle John, and all the others. I've really missed them," Mandie said. "It seems like we've been gone an awfully long time. Why, my little brother has probably grown so much by now, I won't know him."

"I've missed my mother, too," Celia said.

Jonathan raised his dark eyebrows and said, "Well, traveling around the world is old stuff to me."

Mandie looked at him and said solemnly, "Maybe you and your father can work out better arrangements, and you'll be able to stay home in New York and go to school."

"Maybe," Jonathan said wistfully, avoiding the girls' gaze.

Mandie sighed and said, "I suppose my grandmother is just fed up with our adventures. Where will you go now, Jonathan?"

"I'll go back to London with you people and wait for my father there, or at least a message from him telling me what to do," Jonathan said.

"I just remembered Uncle Ned is back at the hotel," Mandie said. "I have something I want to talk to him about."

"About seeing the leprechaun?" Jonathan asked with his mischievous grin.

Mandie looked at him and said sternly, "What I talk to

Uncle Ned about is none of your business." Then she quickly thought better of the remark and apologized. "I'm sorry, Jonathan. I guess I'm just upset about Molly."

"It's all right," Jonathan told her.

"Here comes your grandmother, Mandie, and it looks like she has a lot of packages," Celia said.

When the adults entered the carriage, Mandie was surprised to see how many packages her grandmother had. She was curious, but not enough to ask about them now. She was tired and dirty, and just wanted to be home in bed.

Chapter 11 / Decisions Are Made

When they arrived back at the hotel, the three young people had to walk through the lobby and face the stares of the hotel guests. Mrs. Taft had given all of them packages to carry, with orders to go directly to their rooms and take baths in preparation for bed.

She and Senator Morton lingered at the carriage. Mandie wondered if her grandmother was ashamed to be seen with them.

Molly seemed to be only half awake as Mandie held her hand on the way to their bedroom. Celia carried Snowball, and Jonathan ended up with most of the packages, which he dumped into the girls' sitting room. Continuing down the hall to his own room, he called back a tired "Good-night" to the girls.

When they reached their bedroom, Celia hurried to draw a bath for Molly, while Mandie laid Mrs. Taft's purchases out on their bed. Molly slid to the floor, tired and sleepy.

Snowball climbed upon the big bed, curled up and went to sleep. Mandie pulled a long, white lacy nightgown out of a bag, underthings out of another, and two dresses from a box. She also found a pair of shoes in a box.

"Aren't they pretty!" Celia remarked as she returned from the bathroom.

"Pretty, yes, but I do hope they fit, especially the shoes," Mandie said. "Now to get her into the tub." She tried to shake the child awake. "Molly, wake up. We're going to take a nice hot bath."

Molly finally opened her eyes, looked up at Mandie, and as though she had just remembered where she was, jumped to her feet. "Where is me mummy?" she asked.

"Remember? She was hurt, and the firemen took her to the hospital," Mandie said. "Now, let's take off these dirty clothes and get into the tub." She quickly pulled the torn, dirty dress over the child's head.

"But I will get cold if ye take me dress," Molly said.

Celia, watching, said, "Mandie, I would imagine she has never had a real bath. I didn't see a bathtub in their house."

Molly looked at Celia and asked, "A bathtub? What might that be?"

"Here, we'll show you," Mandie said as she led the child into the bathroom.

Molly looked at the huge tub, ran her hand through the water, and asked, "Ye be expectin' me to swim in that water?"

Mandie smiled and said, "Oh, so you know how to swim. Would you believe I don't know how to swim, and I'm a lot older than you are. Come on, I'll lift you in." Molly allowed Mandie to pick her up and carefully sit her down in the tub of water.

Molly looked around inside the tub. She paddled the

water with her fingers, then smiled and said, "This water be feelin' good, it does."

"That's good," Mandie said with a sigh of relief. "Now we have to wash your hair first. Like this. Bend your head over and I'll wash it all clean and shiny. Then we'll wash the rest of you, and then we have a nice, white lacy night-gown to be put on."

"For me?" Molly asked.

"For you," Mandie said. "My grandmother bought it for you."

Molly was curious about everything, but she allowed Mandie to wash her hair and give her a good bath.

When they were finished, and Celia came in with the nightgown, Molly was delirious with joy. She had never seen such a beautiful garment, much less owned one.

As Mandie put it on her and buttoned it up, Molly asked, "And what work do I be havin' to do for this?"

Mandie and Celia looked at each other.

"You don't have to work for this, Molly, or all the other pretty things my grandmother bought for you. We gave them to you because we love you," Mandie tried to ex-plain. "Now, come on and see what else we have for you."

Celia began holding up the other things on the bed, and Molly's eyes grew round with wonder. She stuttered in an effort to speak.

"Now we're going to hang these up. Tomorrow morn-ing you can decide which dress you will wear," Mandie told her. "But right now you have to go to bed and sleep."

Mandie thought Molly would sleep with her and Celia, but Mrs. Taft came through the sitting room, looked into their bedroom, and said, "Get blankets and make up this settee in the sitting room for Molly, Amanda. And leave your door open so you can hear her if she gets up during the night."

"The things you bought for her are beautiful," Mandie remarked.

Molly, listening to their conversation, raced to Mrs. Taft and hugged her around the legs. "I thank ye with all me heart, I do. Niver in me born days have I had such lovelies," Molly said, looking up at Mrs. Taft.

The girls watched and smiled as Mrs. Taft, uncomfortable with all the affection, tried to move away from the child. "They're all yours, Molly. Now go to bed and sleep. Good-night, girls." Mrs. Taft quickly but gently removed Molly's hands from around her, and planted a kiss on top of the little girl's head. As Mrs. Taft left the room for her own, Mandie and Celia bid her good-night.

"I'll get the blankets, Mandie, if you want to take your bath first," Celia offered.

Mandie laughed as she looked at herself in the looking glass. "I suppose I am dirtier than you. Thanks. I'll hurry, Celia," she said as she found clean nightclothes and went into the bathroom.

She thought about Molly's problem while she washed her hair and took her bath. How could she find out whether Molly had any relatives? Maybe the child would know, but she rather doubted that, since she seemed to drift all over town without anyone looking after her.

Even though Mandie hurried, Molly was asleep by the time she finished. After Celia bathed and washed her hair, the girls sat on their bed and rubbed their hair with large bath towels, then brushed each other's hair until it was completely dry.

"Well, we never got to the river," Celia remarked. "To take that boat ride, I mean."

"It doesn't matter to me," Mandie said, crawling into the big bed and shoving Snowball down to the foot. "I am wondering, Celia, how we can find out if Molly has any relatives."

"Maybe she can tell us," Celia said as she got under the covers on her side of the bed. "She said her father was dead, so maybe she knows other things about her family."

Mandie sat up and said, "I just remembered something. That fireman knew who Molly was. Maybe he would know about her family, if we can find him somehow. I imagine Senator Morton would be able to locate him." She yawned and lay back down. "Mmmm, I'm sleepy. Good-night."

Celia didn't answer. She had already fallen asleep. As Mandie began to drift off, she remembered that she should reprimand Molly for stealing that candy in the shop, but decided with all the child's misfortune she would postpone it until some other time. Then Mandie almost sat up in bed when she suddenly remembered that they were going home soon. She may not have an opportunity to talk to Molly about it.

The next morning, Mandie was wakened by Molly as she crept into the bed with her and Celia. This woke Snowball, too, and he crawled up onto his mistress's pillow.

"What is it?" Mandie asked as she quickly sat up to see what was going on.

"I got cold out there all by meself," Molly told her as she pulled the covers up around her.

Mandie smiled and said, "That's all right. I think it's time to get up anyway." She yawned and stretched until Celia woke up and did likewise.

Celia sat up and said, "Mandie, if we're going home, we have to pack our things, don't you think?" She swung her feet off the side of the bed and looked at the clock on the table. "Seven o'clock," she added.

Molly sat up in the bed and asked, "Ye be goin' home?"

"Soon," Mandie said as she jumped out of bed. "Right now we have to get dressed and find out what my grandmother plans on doing today."

Molly instantly sprang out of bed. "Kin I put on a new dress?" she asked as she pulled at Mandie's nightgown to get her attention.

"Of course, Molly," Mandie said, going over to the wardrobe and taking down the two new dresses. "Which one do you want to wear?"

Molly looked over each detail of the lacy, frilly dresses as she hopped on one foot and then the other. "I want both of 'em," she declared.

"Both of them belong to you, but you can only wear one at a time. Which will it be?" Mandie asked her again. "The white one, or the blue one?"

"What color dress will ye be wearin' today?" Molly asked.

"I suppose I'll wear my blue voile," Mandie told her.

"Then I'll be puttin' on the blue one, too," Molly said with a big grin.

Celia got up and helped Molly get dressed. Mandie found the shoes a little large, but a good enough fit that Molly could wear them. She brushed Molly's carrot-red hair until it shone like gold. When the girls had finished with her, they stood her in front of the tall looking glass.

Molly's eyes widened and her mouth fell open. "That be me in that lookin' glass?" she asked.

"It sure is," Mandie said, grinning at the little girl's obvious pleasure. Then she asked, "Molly, you never did tell us your other name. What is it? Do you know?"

"Me mither named me Molly and that's it. I told you," Molly said, prancing around the room.

"But everyone has two names. My name is Mandie Shaw and Celia's is Celia Hamilton. So you see, you

should have another name. You don't know what it is?"
Mandie asked again.

Molly stopped and looked at her. "I don't be havin'
one. I'll just be Molly and have Shaw for my other name
like you."

Mandie stooped and embraced the little girl. She
smelled fresh and clean.

"I'll let you use my other name then," Mandie told her.
"I love you."

Molly smiled and shyly ducked her head.

Through the open bedroom door, the girls saw Mrs.
Taft come in from the hallway. Mandie was surprised to
see her fully dressed, apparently already having been out
somewhere.

"Grandmother, you've been out already? We're all
ready for breakfast," Mandie told her.

Mrs. Taft sat down in a big chair. "Amanda, the boat
that we need to get back to England only sails every other
day from here. Therefore, we will not be leaving until early
tomorrow morning. I want you and Celia and Jonathan
to have your things packed and ready to go by six o'clock
in the morning."

Mandie and Celia stood still, listening solemnly. Molly
had backed away into a corner.

"Yes, ma'am," Celia said.

"We'll be ready, Grandmother," Mandie told her.
"What are we going to do about Molly?"

"Senator Morton is out checking on some things right
now, and he should join us shortly for breakfast. Now,
let's go down to the dining room," Mrs. Taft said as she
rose.

"What about Uncle Ned and Jonathan?" Mandie
asked.

"They are with Senator Morton," her grandmother

explained as they all walked down the corridor. Mandie left Snowball in their room.

Molly was awed with the idea of sitting down "proper-like" to a table and ordering anything she wanted to eat.

As soon as the waiter brought their coffee, the men and Jonathan joined them. Jonathan sat between the girls, and Molly was at the end of the table with the adults on the other side.

"Did y'all find out anything?" Mandie asked Senator Morton.

"Yes, and it's not too good," he began as the waiter poured his coffee. He glanced at Molly, who was evidently enjoying herself and not paying any attention to the conversation. "They are not sure of her survival," he said in hushed tones. "She will at least be permanently disabled."

"Oh!" Mandie gasped. What will happen to—"

"It seems this woman is not her mother. The child's mother died when she was a baby. The woman, who was the mother's best friend, took her in, rather than putting her in an institution," the senator explained quietly.

Everyone around the table listened to Senator Morton, except Molly, who was still distracted with the china and silver and linen napkin. Mandie's heart beat faster when she realized what this all could mean for Molly.

"Well, what are we going to do?" Mandie asked again, looking to her grandmother and Uncle Ned.

"An institution is the only solution, unless we could find someone to take her in," Senator Morton answered.

"No, no!" Mandie cried, realizing that Molly's attention was drawn to her at that instant. She lowered her voice and continued, "Please, Grandmother, do something, anything but that." She looked imploringly at Uncle Ned.

Mrs. Taft finally spoke, "Amanda, the authorities are

searching for information about an aunt in the United States. If they find her name and address, we'll take her to the aunt." She glanced at Molly who had begun eating a roll and butter.

Mandie's face broke into smiles as she said, "Grandmother, that's wonderful! They've just got to locate her. What can we do to help them?"

"Nothing I know of, Amanda," Mrs. Taft replied as the food was being served.

"Grandmother, if they don't locate her before we leave, couldn't we take her with us, and find thé aunt after we get home?" Mandie asked, eagerly leaning forward.

"Amanda, I don't know what we would do with her in the meantime," Mrs. Taft said. "You will be away at school as soon as we get back, and I already have Hilda to look after."

"Oh, but I'm sure my mother would love having her at home. She'd be good to play with my baby brother," Mandie declared, smiling.

Mrs. Taft immediately dropped her eyes and reached for her handkerchief. She delicately touched it to her nose.

Mandie noticed and said, "Grandmother, I hope you're not getting a cold."

Senator Morton looked at Mandie and then at Mrs. Taft. Even Uncle Ned seemed quiet all of a sudden.

"No, dear, I don't have a cold. Now, let's eat our breakfast," Mrs. Taft said, pocketing the handkerchief and picking up her fork. But she wouldn't look straight at Mandie again.

Mandie, thinking her grandmother was disgusted with her adventures, said, "Grandmother, if I've caused you any trouble on this trip, I'm really and truly sorry. And I hope you've decided to go home tomorrow because you want to and not because of me."

Mrs. Taft cleared her throat and said sternly, "Amanda, eat your breakfast."

"Yes, Grandmother," Mandie said and picked up her fork.

Celia and Jonathan looked at Mandie as they also began eating. Molly was eagerly devouring everything on her plate, oblivious to all that was going on around her.

After everyone was finished with the meal, Mrs. Taft told them, "We will all stay around the hotel today. We won't be doing any more sightseeing. That way, if the authorities try to get in touch with us they'll be able to find us."

She rose to leave, and everyone else followed.

Mandie looked up at Uncle Ned across the table and said, "Uncle Ned, I need to talk to you."

Everyone turned to look at her, but the old Cherokee smiled and said, "Now? We go to front yard, Papoose."

"Thanks, Uncle Ned," she said, and turning to Celia she asked, "Would you and Jonathan take care of Molly for a little while? Please don't let her run away."

Molly was listening and said, "I don't be wantin' to run away. I want to keep my pretty clothes, and I like the food, too."

Everyone smiled at her and Mandie stooped to embrace her. "Then you behave, and I'll see you in a little while."

"Yes, ma'am," she said, trying to speak properly.

Everyone laughed again. Mandie said, "I suppose I must be getting old when someone calls me ma'am."

Mandie followed Uncle Ned outside to the courtyard where they sat on the low wall in the bright morning sunshine. She wanted to talk to him about what she had seen in the cellar, but she didn't want him to doubt her.

"Uncle Ned, I want to tell you something that you might not believe," Mandie began, glancing up at him.

"First, I want to tell Papoose," Uncle Ned said, "I sorry I not go last night. Papoose almost die in fire, and I not there to help. I promised Jim Shaw when he go to happy hunting ground, I watch over Papoose. Last night, I not watch. Forgive me." He reached out to hold her hand.

Mandie looked up at him in amazement. Uncle Ned never did anything wrong. He was always trying to keep her feet on the straight and narrow path. Now he was apologizing to her because he had taken the time to rest instead of going with her to the river.

"Uncle Ned, you haven't done anything wrong. There's nothing for me to forgive you for," Mandie protested as she smiled at him.

"No, I break promise to Jim Shaw, and Papoose almost get hurt," he insisted. "Everybody does wrong. No body perfect. But everybody must ask forgiveness for wrong. Try to do better next time."

Mandie squeezed his hand with hers and said, "I love you so much, Uncle Ned, and in my eyes you can do no wrong."

Uncle Ned shook his head and said firmly, "Until Papoose gets back home, I stay with her. No more visits to friends. No more extra rest. I go where Papoose go."

"All right, Uncle Ned. I always love having you with me. You always know how to solve problems and situations I get into," Mandie said, standing up. "Now, I have something to tell you. I don't think it's a problem, but it's a mystery. I want to show you something first. Come this way."

Mandie led the old Indian around the hotel to the door going into the cellar. When she stopped, Uncle Ned looked at the door and then at her.

"This door opens onto steps going down to the cellar. I'll show you," Mandie said, pushing the door open and stepping back. "Look inside, Uncle Ned."

Uncle Ned did as she asked, and then he looked at her again.

"Well, it was like this. You see, Snowball always runs away when he gets the chance, and yesterday as we were preparing to get into the carriage out front, he got away and ran in here," Mandie said, pausing to see if the old man was listening.

"Snowball went in cellar?" Uncle Ned asked. "And Papoose go after him?"

Mandie smiled. "That's right. He ran inside and disappeared and I was going after him. I got down to the landing and I heard a noise. Then I saw a little man, in green clothes—"

Uncle Ned interrupted her with a laugh as he said, "Fairy? Papoose see fairy?"

"He must have been a leprechaun, Uncle Ned. He was dressed just like the actors were in the play. He looked at me and I looked at him, and then he just evaporated, and Snowball came running out as if a dog were chasing him, with his fur all raised up," she explained.

Uncle Ned nodded and said, "Must have been fairy. Animals afraid of fairies." He smiled.

Mandie looked up at him, wondering whether he was serious.

"I saw fairy, too," Uncle Ned told her. "Walking down hall in hotel."

"Walking down the hall in the hotel?" Mandie repeated in disbelief. "You saw one, too?"

"Yes. Fairy dressed for play," he explained.

Mandie drew in her breath sharply, as it dawned on

Snyder County Library
Selinsgrove, PA 17870

her that Uncle Ned was saying he saw one of the actors in the play.

"Are you sure, Uncle Ned?" Mandie asked.

"Yes. He tell man at desk, 'Come to play,' " Uncle Ned said.

"Well, if it was an actor I saw, what was he doing in the cellar?" Mandie asked.

"Keep things for play in cellar," Uncle Ned said.

"Oh, you mean the stuff they use on the stage." Mandie's disappointment showed on her face. "Well, shucks! I thought I had seen a real leprechaun," she said with a loud sigh.

Uncle Ned smiled at her as they turned to walk back around the hotel. "Keep watch. Maybe you see real one." He put his arm around her shoulder and squeezed her tight.

They walked through the front door and saw Mrs. Taft and Senator Morton sitting in an alcove talking to two men in uniforms. Mandie tugged at Uncle Ned's hand to hurry him across the room with her to see what was going on.

As they approached, Mrs. Taft said, "Sit down a minute, Uncle Ned, Amanda. These are the authorities in charge of Molly right now."

Mandie sat down nearest to the man who was doing the talking, and Mrs. Taft introduced her granddaughter. The men had met Uncle Ned earlier that morning.

"Please, can't we just take Molly with us and find the aunt after we get back home?" Mandie begged, her blue eyes focused on the man.

"That's what we have decided, lass," the man said, with a big smile. "We have given your grandmother the name and address of the child's aunt, and she will locate the woman there. In the meantime, we are getting papers ready for Molly to go to America with you."

Mandie reached up to squeeze the man's hand. "Oh, thank you. I'm so glad she won't have to go to an orphanage."

"Yawl are solving a big problem for us, that's for sure," the man said. "And we be thankful for it."

"What about the woman that Molly was living with? Will she be all right?" Mandie asked.

"We don't be knowin' that right now," the man said. "But we'll stay in touch."

Mandie suddenly remembered to ask, "What is Molly's last name? She didn't know."

"Her name is Molly Ritchie. Her father was a law officer here in Belfast, and he died suddenly of an incurable disease when Molly was about two months old. The mother didn't live long after that. She was thrown from a horse. Missus Wiley took Molly in."

"I'm so glad to know all this, so I can tell Molly," Mandie said.

Mrs. Taft told her, "They will also give us her birth certificate. She will be seven years old on September first."

"We must go now, madam, sirs," the man said as he and his fellow officer rose and nodded to Uncle Ned and Senator Morton. "We will be back when all the papers are ready, and if you are not available we will leave them at the desk for you."

"Oh, thank you so much," Mandie said as she stood up. "And, sir, please let us know about Mrs. Wiley."

"That we will, and we would like to know that Molly is settled, too," he said as he and the other man turned to leave.

"Sit down a minute, Amanda," Mrs. Taft said. "Please."

Mandie took one look at her grandmother and could

see a lecture coming. She sat on the edge of her chair and waited.

"Amanda, this will be a particularly hard journey for me back across the ocean when we leave London, and I want you to promise me that you will take complete charge of Molly, and that you and Celia will not create any trouble on the way," Mrs. Taft said.

"Are you sick, Grandmother?" Mandie was worried. She noticed Mrs. Taft looked pale and seemed awfully nervous.

"No, no, dear, I'm not sick, just tired. Now go find your friends. They're in the park in the back. And, please, behave yourself. We'll meet back in the dining room for the noon meal. In the meantime, don't leave the hotel property," Mrs. Taft said.

"Yes, Grandmother," Mandie said as she walked down the corridor toward the back door.

At least the problem with Molly was solved. Mandie was happy about that. But she felt bad about something she couldn't put her finger on. Her grandmother seemed upset, and she thought it was because of her. She would really and truly try to behave herself from now on.

Chapter 12 / Homeward Bound

Before daylight the next morning, Molly had wakened the girls as she pranced around the bedroom. She was dripping with happiness. Mandie had been afraid she would create a fuss when she was told she'd be going to the United States with them. Instead, she was overjoyed, and when she heard about the aunt there, she talked about nothing else. And Mandie discovered that Molly knew the woman she had been living with was not her mother, but she was the only mother Molly ever knew.

The girls were glad to be up early so that they could get their things packed.

Mrs. Taft opened the door to her bedroom and looked across the sitting room to the girls' room. "I'm glad to see y'all are up. Let's get dressed now and go to breakfast. We don't want to miss that boat to England."

"Yes, ma'am," Mandie said. "It won't take us but a few minutes more to be ready."

After breakfast, they took the boat and crossed the

Irish Sea to England. Then Mrs. Taft hurried them on to their hotel. As soon as the walked into the lobby, she rushed them to their rooms.

"We have to find out about the schedule to go home," she told the young people as she and Senator Morton went toward the front desk. "Go to your rooms, but don't unpack until I find out when we'll be leaving for home."

Uncle Ned joined Mrs. Taft and the senator, and the three young people, with Molly in tow, started to walk toward the rooms they had occupied before, when someone called Jonathan's name. They all looked across the lobby toward a well-dressed gentleman sitting in an alcove.

"Jonathan!" he called again as he stood up.

"Father!" Jonathan answered, dropping his bags on the floor and running toward the man.

Tears came in Mandie's eyes as she watched the man put an arm around his son and motion him to a seat. Jonathan pointed to his luggage and came hurrying back to retrieve it.

A huge smile spread across his face as he told the girls, "It's my father! I can't believe my father is here!"

"I'm glad, Jonathan. We'll catch up with you later," Mandie told him.

"And I am happy for you, too, Jonathan," Celia added.

Molly stood there listening and looking. Then she said, "His father is in this world."

"Yes, Molly. He's the only one of us that has a father that is alive," Mandie told her as she pictured her own father's face in her mind. "Come on. We have to go to our rooms now."

After a while, Mandie was beginning to think everyone had forgotten about them. She wondered what was taking the adults so long. Finally Jonathan knocked on their door, and Mandie opened it.

He looked very happy as he managed to say, "You are all to come down to the dining room. Everyone is there. Right away, your grandmother said."

"Let me put Snowball in the bathroom," Mandie said as she turned back into the room. "Celia, Molly, we have to go to the dining room now. Jonathan is here for us." She quickly picked up Snowball and deposited him on the bathroom floor and closed the door. "Come on. Let's go."

Jonathan had not waited for them, so the girls hurried to the dining room where they found everyone at a big table set in a corner.

Mandie was anxious to see and speak to Jonathan's father, about whom she had heard so much. When she, Celia, and Molly walked to the table, Mr. Guyer rose to shake hands with them.

The man was of medium height, stocky, like Jonathan, and when a big grin spread across his face Mandie could see that Jonathan was the image of his father.

"I'm pleased to meet you, Miss Amanda, Miss Celia, and Miss Molly," he shook each one's hand and stooped to smile at Molly.

"I'm glad to meet you, Mr. Guyer. You look just like Jonathan, except older, of course," Mandie told him. She studied his face as they sat down.

Mr. Guyer laughed and said, "You mean Jonathan looks like me?"

"Yes, sir," Mandie agreed with a smile. "And I'm so glad you finally caught up with us."

"So am I. My schedule kept changing, and I was beginning to think I'd have to tell the President himself that I simply had to take time to catch up with my son," he told her.

Mandie raised her eyebrows. "The President?" she asked.

"My father has been on a special mission for President McKinley. That's why he's been gone so long around the world," Jonathan proudly explained.

"But it's all finished now and we can go home," Mr. Guyer said, looking at his son with a smile.

"Lindall, it's time you settled down," Senator Morton said.

"Yes, and take time to enjoy being with your son before he grows up and leaves you," Mrs. Taft told him.

"My business is finished, and I intend to stay in New York so Jonathan can at last make some friends there and go to school," Mr. Guyer replied.

"This secret government business has been a burden. I couldn't even tell my own son the reason for not being able to settle down with him anywhere. But now it's over, and he knows the whole story." He smiled at Jonathan.

"But we are going to Paris and visit there until school starts, aren't we?" Jonathan asked.

"Of course. Your aunt and uncle have finished their mission with our government in Europe, and they'll be returning to New York within the next few months, but we'll visit with them until it's time to enroll you in a school in New York."

Mandie was listening to all this, and her heart was overflowing with joy for Jonathan.

"All my friends here—Mandie, Celia, and Uncle Ned are all coming to New York to visit us sometime soon," Jonathan told his father.

"You are?" Mrs. Taft asked in surprise. "We'll have to let you know later, Jonathan, whether or not they can visit you."

Mandie looked at her grandmother in surprise. Then she realized that Mrs. Taft hadn't been around when the young people were talking and making plans to visit one another.

"Oh, you must come, all of you," Mr. Guyer insisted. "We have a house with so many rooms we don't even use all of them. Please come."

"We'll let you know, Lindall," Mrs. Taft said, a bit uneasily.

Then Mandie remembered that she had learned on their way to Europe that her grandmother and the senator were old friends of Lindall Guyer. Maybe they were not good friends. Maybe there was some reason her grandmother didn't want to visit Mr. Guyer.

The waiter came to the table with coffee.

They had had snacks on the long boat ride from Ireland, but Mandie realized she was really hungry now.

The orders were taken and the waiter left. A sudden silence fell over the group. Even little Molly looked inquiringly from one to the other.

Mandie cleared her throat and asked, "Grandmother, when are we sailing for home?"

"I'm sorry, dear," Mrs. Taft said, looking at her. "I forgot you and Celia weren't here when we got the schedule. As you know, we own a ship line, and we can more or less tell them when we want to go. I contacted the office here, and they are getting a ship ready to sail at dawn tomorrow. So you young people can all relax until then, but please be sure you don't leave the hotel, because the schedule could be moved up sooner. Do you understand?" She looked at Celia and Molly too.

"Yes, ma'am," Mandie replied. "I'll be glad to get back home to my mother and Uncle John and my little brother Samuel." She sighed. "The journey over was exciting, but the one back is going to seem to take forever because I'm in a hurry to get home now."

"Yes, dear, so am I," Mrs. Taft said as she looked seriously at Mandie. "So am I." There was sudden silence around the table again.

Celia broke it this time. "I'll be awfully glad to get home, too, Mrs. Taft. I've really enjoyed this opportunity to see Europe, and I thank you so much, but I've missed my mother."

"I know, dear," Mrs. Taft said. "First of all, you and I'll take Amanda home, and then we'll get you started toward your home in Virginia."

Mandie wondered why Mrs. Taft was not taking them to her home in Asheville, where Celia could get a train home. Then she remembered Celia's mother would not want her to travel alone. Someone would have to go with her. Maybe her grandmother was going to see her home.

The food was served, and everyone ate in silence. Even Molly was quiet and shy around so many strangers.

As she ate, Mandie remembered the friends they had made on the ship coming to England from home. They had met two sisters, Violet and Lily, who were Americans going to England to live with relatives. Mrs. Taft had promised to look them up when she and Mandie and Celia returned to London, en route home.

"Grandmother, are we going to see Violet and Lily while we're here?" she asked.

Mrs. Taft frowned slightly and said, "I don't believe we have time, dear. I don't know how long it would take to locate them, or how long it might take them to come to the hotel. We wouldn't have time to go out into the country to visit them. I'm sorry."

"That's all right, Grandmother," Mandie replied. "I'll write them a letter and explain when I get home."

It was a disjointed round of conversation, as no one seemed to want to talk when Mandie tried to keep things going after each little remark.

Maybe everyone is just tired, Mandie thought.

She turned to Jonathan and asked, "When are you

and your father going to Paris?"

"Tomorrow morning, probably the same time you leave for the United States," he told her. "Wish you could come with me. Just to stir things up a little, you know," he said with his mischievous smile. "I'm sure going to miss you and Celia."

"Thank you, but I had enough of Paris, what with getting kidnapped and all," Celia told him.

"But that's over. We'd be staying at my aunt's house," Jonathan told her.

"What do you mean that's over, Jonathan?" Mandie asked.

"My father has completed his job for the President," Jonathan said. "Those people who kidnapped me were hoping to use me to get information from my father, but it didn't work. And that's all over with now."

"Yes," Mandie said, "but you're forgetting one thing. That strange woman from the ship has been following us all over Europe. We saw her in Ireland, too, remember? She's still around somewhere."

"Oh, I imagine she's just strange," Jonathan said, shrugging his shoulders.

"I hope that's all. I'm tired of having her spy on us everywhere we go," Mandie said.

Mr. Guyer had been listening to the conversation and said, "When Jonathan ran away from home, we thought at first he had been kidnapped, but, as you all know, he had merely run away. Those kidnappers got the kidnapping idea from hearing the news about Jonathan. They figured if they could somehow hold him they would have leverage over me, but it didn't work out that way."

"Thank goodness!" Mandie said with a sigh.

Mrs. Taft spoke to Uncle Ned, who had been completely silent. "If you feel up to a walk, Uncle Ned, it would be all right for the young people to go with you, provided you don't venture too far away from the hotel," she told him.

"Good," Uncle Ned said. "I like walk. I take Papoose and friends with me."

Everyone finished eating, and Uncle Ned stood and looked at Mandie and her friends. "Papoose coming?" he asked.

"Oh, yes, Uncle Ned," Mandie said, jumping up from the table and helping Molly down from her chair.

"I'll go, too," Celia said, joining them. The girls looked at Jonathan, and Jonathan looked at his father.

"Go ahead, Jonathan. The walk will do you good. Mrs. Taft, Senator Morton, and I have some business to talk about anyway," Mr. Guyer told him with a smile.

"Thanks, Father. We won't be gone long," Jonathan said as he left the table and joined the others.

Mandie insisted that she run and get Snowball. She would feed him later.

When she returned with him, they walked outside around the hotel grounds and then down the street. Everyone was tired and anxious to be on their way tomorrow, so conversation was light, and centered on the scenery around them. Soon Uncle Ned told them it was time to return to the hotel.

"We go back now," Uncle Ned said as they came to a wide intersection a short distance from the hotel.

Molly had trouble keeping up with the others, so Uncle Ned picked her up and carried her on his shoulder, which she seemed to enjoy.

When they returned to the hotel, the desk clerk stopped them to say that Mrs. Taft and the others were waiting for them in a little parlor at the end of the corridor.

As they walked toward the parlor, Mandie wondered

why everyone would be waiting together for them. Maybe the ship was ready to sail.

When they came to the doorway of the parlor, the first person Mandie noticed was the strange woman from the ship. She was sitting on a settee between Mrs. Taft and Mr. Guyer, nonchalantly drinking coffee. Mandie gasped in surprise, as did Celia and Jonathan behind her. They all stopped in the doorway to stare.

"Come on in, dear," Mrs. Taft said. "All of you. I want to introduce you to someone. She has been following us all over Europe. She's—"

Mandie interrupted, picking up Snowball and securing him tightly. "Following us is right! She even kidnapped us once, remember? And now she's sitting here with y'all, sipping coffee as though nothing ever happened?"

The strange woman smiled at Mandie.

"Amanda! Amanda!" Mrs. Taft reprimanded her sternly. "Please don't interrupt until I am finished. This is Miss Lucretia Wham. She is a lady detective. She was looking out for all your best interests. When she located Jonathan on the ship, she notified his father, and he had her follow us to be sure Jonathan was safe."

"And I almost failed in Paris, dear," Miss Wham said as she set down her coffee cup. "Then I had to resort to strict measures to protect you girls by taking you into protective custody at that house. But you were too smart for me and escaped."

Everything began to fall into place. Mandie, Celia, and Jonathan sat down on a settee opposite the woman. Uncle Ned sat in a chair in the corner with Molly and listened.

"Why didn't you tell us who you were?" Mandie asked, watching the woman closely.

"Because President McKinley asked me not to, dear, for security reasons," Miss Wham explained as she adjusted the diamond broach at her throat.

She was still wearing the same expensive-looking black dress and flashy diamond rings on her wrinkled hands. Mandie thought she looked awfully old to be a lady detective. She had gray hair and sharp black eyes, and she was even shorter than Mandie.

"You don't look like a detective," Mandie said, not able to express her surprise any other way.

"That's what makes me valuable to my kind of job. No one would ever suspect a little old lady like me to be a detective," Miss Wham told her.

Later, in their room, Mandie remarked to Celia, "Looks like everyone has been working for President McKinley. And we weren't smart enough to figure it out," she said.

"Well, how could we when we've never been involved in any such thing before?" Celia reasoned.

Molly was already asleep in bed, while the girls continued to rehash the facts they had learned upon returning to London.

"You know, Celia, I just remembered something today that I had almost forgotten," Mandie told her. "Remember when my grandmother and I had an awful argument about my father because he was half Cherokee? It was when we were in Belgium."

"What does that have to do with the little old lady?" Celia asked.

"Nothing," Mandie said. "It just seems to me that my grandmother began to get perturbed about all our adventures from that time on. She seems to have changed recently, probably because she's just plain worn out with it all. Do you think I ought to talk to her about it?"

Celia thought for a moment and then said, "No, Mandie, I would wait at least until things quiet down. You don't want to stir something up. Just be as sweet and nice as you can be on our trip home, so you don't irritate your grandmother."

Mandie smiled at her friend and said, "I'll try to, but sometimes I don't believe I know how. My imagination works faster than my common sense."

When the girls finally went to bed, Mandie slept almost immediately and dreamed of home. She usually dreamed of her father, who had died the year before, but tonight she had dreams of her mother, her baby brother, and her Uncle John, whom her mother had married after Mandie's father died.

Mandie could hear the baby crying in her dream and could see her mother rocking him. Suddenly, she could hear him screaming. Then her mother was screaming, too.

Mandie awoke abruptly, her heart racing and her body shivering, even though she had broken out in a sweat. The dream had been so real.

She tossed and turned trying to sleep again because she knew they would sail in the morning and they had to be up early.

Reminding herself that it wouldn't be too much longer before she was back home with her mother, her baby brother, and Uncle John, she stopped worrying about them and her grandmother's sudden decision to return home, and finally fell asleep again.

THEY'RE HOT!

**Mandie Fans
will love preparing
Mandie's delicious
recipes from the past!**

FREE!!
Mandie Apron & Bonnet
Pattern Included in
Mandie's Cookbook

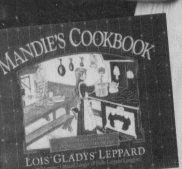

MANDIE'S COOKBOOK

LOIS GLADYS LEPPARD